ESCAPE of the CHAMELEON

This book is a work of fiction. Names, characters, places, and incidents either are products of the author's imagination or are used fictitiously. Any resemblance to actual persons, living or dead, events, or locales is entirely coincidental.

Escape of the Chameleon

© **2012, Verna Elliott Hutlet**
ISBN 978-0-9917868-4-8

Hutlet, Verna Elliott.

Escape of the Chameleon / Verna Elliott Hutlet

1. Fiction 2. Mystery

First Edition

10 9 8 7 6 5 4 3 2 1

For those who have listened to my stories throughout the years.
Let me take you on another adventure.

For my husband & best friend, Herby
Our six wonderful children,
Tammy, Mark, Lauri, Joanne, Jay, Jacalyn
their partners & our beautiful grandchildren
&
for my sisters & brother

Stone-peppered hills cupped the old farmyard like wheat in a weathered palm, their shadows ill defining the buildings in the hollow below. *Those in sunlight can be seen before those in shadow.* Such was the reasoning behind Tony McTavish's purchase of the property. William watched her descend the sunlit side of the hill, his hand instinctively reaching across his chest to check the revolver beneath his jacket. He monitored her maze-like approach like a cougar vigilant on a deer, having become conditioned long ago to scrutinizing anything that moved.

For a moment, he visioned another girl; Elizabeth, flittering like a butterfly through unkept grasses above the industrial quarter of a small Irish town. The two had hidden time and time again in those tall, protective grasses; a boy prisoner and a girl sympathizer trying to plan a way out of hell. William sighed, still weary from mourning her. Elizabeth would be alive today if not for him.

The young woman was closer now, strands of dark auburn hair freed from the tie-back, which had once held her hair orderly. She approached the vine-covered veranda where William cautiously waited in the shadows.

Liberty Enns stood nervously at the base of the steps to the veranda, somewhat embarrassed at his unwillingness to step forward into the sunlight. She offered up a food container. "I'm very sorry about your father's passing...My Mom thought you may use a pie." It was an old-fashioned custom in the rural community to pay respects to the grieving family with an offer of food.

William had never experienced anything remotely neighborly in his life. He hesitated, and so she opened the container to free the aroma of freshly baked Saskatoon berry. She did not notice William's hand instinctively slip once again beneath his jacket to envelope the trigger of the gun.

Tony and William had moved from Ireland to seek seclusion in the Canadian Midwest and did not welcome visitors. Past experience had spoiled William's ability to trust, and so he remained rigid, calculating the possibility of deception before accepting the pie. A black and white Border Collie hugged her pant leg, tail wagging and eyes intent on the pie. William determined that the dog offered little threat, being obviously more interested in the pie than William's hand on the concealed weapon. As for the lady, well, humans were not as transparent as canine.

William approached the stairs, aware that his manners were lagging. "Thanks...Would ye be wanting a cool drink. It's a long walk over the hills." There was a slight Irish accent to his voice.

Liberty graciously accepted and followed him into the house. She was naturally a bit curious about her secretive neighbors. She noted the kitchen was neat, the walls barren except for one calendar pinned to the wall. William bent over to place the pie on a refrigerator shelf and for the flick of a second, his jacket fell open, revealing a gun tucked in a shoulder holster. Liberty instantly glanced away so as not to let him know she had seen the weapon. Her breathing quickened and she scanned the room for exits, fearful that she had walked into a lion's den.

He turned to her, "Water, soft drink, beer?"

"A soft drink would be nice". Her voice cracked unnaturally and she coughed to hide her uneasiness. She pulled out a chair closest to the door exit and seated herself at the table.

He returned with two cola cans and two glasses filled with ice.
"I'm Liberty," she said. "Mike and Donna Enn's daughter." She gestured with her hands, "...over the hills to the east."

He nodded. "William!" was all he offered in response.

Liberty had not seen William before. Tony McTavish occasionally bought groceries in town but William never accompanied him. William was a good looking man. His short, light brown hair feathered softly back from his handsome face, revealing two sapphire eyes that could probably cut right to the truth if you ever thought to lie to him. Liberty diverted her green eyes for fear he might comprehend how handsome she thought he was. He was well-built and tanned and looked like he had spent some time in the sun, but she didn't know what at, as the farm held no livestock and no land suitable for tilling. The former owner had raised sheep on the hillsides, but for the past year, it appeared William and Tony McTavish did no farming and made no livelihood. No one could guess how they made a living, but they always paid their bills, so people kept to their own business.

Liberty noted two photographs on a cupboard close to the table where she was seated. One frame held a faded wedding photo, the other, a young boy whom she assumed was William, standing beside Tony McTavish. "You don't resemble your father", she blurted out honestly, noticing the dark features and short stockier build of the older man. "You must take after your mother."

"Tony took me in when my parents died. We're not blood related."

"Oh!" She was surprised, as the community had always regarded them as father and son. "Do you mind me asking what happened to your parents?"

"Accident!"

Her face saddened. "That's too bad! You had no other relatives then?"

"None that wanted to feed me." William's answer was short and to the point. Liberty had the feeling he was a man who spoke volumes with only a few words.

Not knowing how to answer his comment, she offered a comforting thought. "Well... I'm sure Mr. McTavish was happy to have you as a son."

"More as a project."

Liberty tilted her head and her eyes winced in surprise at William's strange opinion of a father figure he had just buried.

"Project?" she questioned, not understanding his strange statement.

William twirled the ice in his glass and said nothing more. He took a large swallow of cola. Liberty wasn't sure whether he looked bitter or sad, or maybe a bit of both. Her shoulders rose and fell with a little sigh. Choosing a safe topic was going to be a problem with this complex man. She glanced towards the exit again, reassuring herself that escape was still possible.

"Do you plan to continue living here...now that Mr. McTavish has passed away...or does your business take you elsewhere?" Liberty bit her tongue the moment the words left her lips. She recalled the old saying, *Curiosity killed the cat*. Perhaps it was not wise to know his business. After all, a man wearing a concealed handgun was obviously not only prepared to use it, but expecting to use it. Her hands trembled slightly, rattling the ice cubes in her glass. She knew he noted her nervousness for his eyes drifted to her hands, which now held a vise-like grip on the drinking glass so that the ice cubes wouldn't dance.

William thought to himself, "The hands of an experienced sniper wouldn't shake like that." His blue eyes raised slowly to observe her face. She had an innocent face with gentle eyes, attractive in her simplicity like still water on a mountain lake. A slight splash of freckles decorated her nose, and William figured a man could easily let his guard down with a girl who had freckles on her nose and a dog who liked pie. Then, realizing the danger of relaxing his attentiveness, he rose to end the conversation and their visitation.

Liberty quickly swallowed a final sip from her glass, relieved to escape towards the door entrance.

He turned to face her in the doorway. "Thank your mother for the pie."

"You're most welcome...Oh, do you go by McTavish?" She was curious as to what his birth name was. Maybe she would do a criminal check on him when she returned home, seeing as he was a neighbor and carried a gun.

"William will do," he said quietly, offering nothing more.

"Well, come visit us sometime," she called politely back to him as she retraced her path to the hills. He lifted a hand in slight response, and turned and walked back into the house.

William went to remove the two glasses from the table, and then halted. There was something comforting about two glasses on the table. It gave the illusion of one not being alone. He pushed the chairs back in place and left the two glasses on the table to fill the empty void in the room. He was weary, his emotions somewhat mixed over the death of Tony. For most of his life, he had tried to escape the man. Now he missed the only person on earth whom he could trust to guard his back.

He removed his jacket and slipped out of his shoulder holster, resting it on the table beside the drinking glasses. He slipped back into his jacket, and like a photographer who repeatedly checks his camera settings, William instinctively pulled the gun from the holster to check its readiness. By doing so, the young man was preoccupied for a few moments, and did not see the shadow approach from behind.

Liberty didn't sigh with relief until she was halfway up the hill towards home. She decided she knew less about her neighbor now than before her visit, but having seen the gun, it was probably in her best interests not to know anything more. Too bad he was so handsome.

The dog kept turning around and staring at the old farmhouse, as if he could hear something she could not. "I wouldn't go hunting gophers on his side of the hill, if I were you, Cleo," she advised the dog." He's scary!"

It took some time for Liberty to climb the hill. Upon reaching the top, she rested on a large stone and glanced back down into the valley. The dog barked, and Liberty silenced him." What's the matter, Cleo? Did you have your heart set on that pie?" The dog trotted back down the hill towards the McTavish household. When Liberty failed to follow, the dog returned obediently to her side, but did not take his eyes off the farm house. An anxious whine escaped his throat.

Distance and afternoon shadows made the old farm house poorly visible from the top of the hill. Liberty squinted her eyes, straining to distinguish what was coming out the front door. Suddenly, a burst of recognizable smoke curled above the rooftop, and Liberty shouted, "Oh no! The house is on fire." She rustled in her pocket for her cell phone and dialed for the fire department.

Dark smoke continued to billow out the front door as Liberty reached the veranda. She shouted William's name but received no answer. Taking a deep breath of fresh air, she peeped inside the kitchen doorway and called again. Flames circled the outer limits of the room and ate across the ceiling with forked reptile tongues. The kitchen was in complete disarray. Chairs were broken and scattered about the room, dishes and appliances smashed to the floor. Even the side cupboard lay tipped on its side. Suddenly, she noticed William lying unconscious on the floor, half hidden behind the overturned table near the doorway. She stepped back and inhaled fresh outdoor air again, then held her breath and darted to his side, shocked to find the young man covered with blood. She did not take time to find out if he was alive or dead. She was struggling for air, so quickly slipped her arms under his shoulders and dragged him through spattered pools of blood towards the open door.

As they approached the door entrance, Liberty noticed the 2 photograph frames on the floor within arm's length of her path. In a moment of compassion, she grabbed and tossed each quickly out the door like skimming pebbles on a river. She had a feeling that in a few minutes, the two photos might be the only things William had left of his past.

Liberty dragged William a safe distance from the house, and then sat exhausted beside him, trying to catch her breath. His breathing was irregular and came in short, quick gasps. At least for the moment, she knew him to be alive. Blood trickled from the edge of William's lips and a large bruise had begun to darken his temple. Liberty brushed his locks aside so she could examine the blow. She wished she had something cold to put on the injury to discourage the swelling. His arms were bloody and had multiple cuts, as if he had used them to defend himself against a knife attack. Fortunately, his suit jacket had protected him somewhat from receiving deeper slashes. Liberty concentrated on his blow to the head and the painful breathing of his chest. His unbuttoned suit jacket lay open and she noted he no longer wore the shoulder holster and gun. She whipped off her own jacket and covered him as best she could, fearing shock would soon set in.

Distant sirens scattered birds into the sky, and Liberty looked at her watch, counting the seconds for the ambulance and fire truck to arrive. She knew both would be coming, as it was customary in the small village for both fire truck and ambulance to respond to emergency calls.

Her cell phone rang. "Yes, I can hear your sirens, Gary. I'm okay... It's William...William McTavish. I dragged him out of his house. He's unconscious from a blow to the head, I think... not from smoke. He looks more...beat up than anything... yes, beat up...I don't know...He was fine when I left him about half an hour ago, but now he's covered in blood...Yes, see you in a few seconds."

William moaned and Liberty bent over close to his beaten face. "Who did this to you?"

William's eyes partly opened and his mind became conscious of her hovering anxiously over him. "Ac...cident. S...stairs!" Then he faded into unconsciousness again. Liberty had seen the condition of the kitchen; the trashed furniture, the blood spattered floor, and his body lying nowhere near the staircase. His wounds were certainly not from a fall down the staircase. Her eyes fearfully circled the farmyard, searching for sign of the intruder who must have done this act. If there was another human being in the vicinity, Liberty felt Cleo would have noticed and barked at him. In fact, she now realized that her dog had heard something from the hilltop, but she had ignored his attempts to bring it to her attention.

Cleo now waited unmoving beside her, his full attention on the train of dust from the fire truck, ambulance and local police detachment storming into the yard. "How did all this happen, Liberty?" Dr. Gary Feddin questioned as he rushed to William's side and bent over to examine his injuries. Constable Joel Fleury kneeled down beside Liberty, the ambulance staff and doctor, waiting for Liberty's answer.

She hesitated. William had worn a gun and must have been expecting trouble. She had a feeling she might put herself and family in danger if she revealed any knowledge about William's business. "He said it was an accident...the stairs," she said truthfully. "I saw the smoke from the hilltop, and when I got here, I dragged him from the fire." Liberty never mentioned the gun or the state of the kitchen. She knew she should submit all evidence, but for now, decided it safer if the attacker thought she had no connection to William. After all, the intruder was still out there somewhere.

As they loaded William into the ambulance, the Fire Chief yelled across to the RCMP Constable. "There's not much we can do to save the house, Joel. It's old. Burnin' like dry timber in a wind."

"Can you tell how it started?"

The Fireman shook his head. "Hard to tell at this point, but I'll scout through it when the fire's out. These old houses are kindling if a fire starts. Burn quick and complete."

"Doesn't look like the boy's having a good day," the Constable sighed somewhat compassionately. "First his father's funeral, now his home gone and everything in it."

"Not quite. I found these." The Fire Chief handed two broken and bloody photo frames to the police officer.
"Oh, I threw those out the door." Liberty reached for the frames. "I'll return them to him."

Constable Fleury frowned. "You took time out from pulling a man from a burning fire to retrieve photos?"

Liberty almost panicked at his skeptical face. "They were close...at my feet...I just grabbed and threw them out the door."

In small towns, everyone knows the other fairly well. Constable Fleury had faith in Liberty's good character, but he was a trained officer and could see William's injuries were suspicious. "Funny the photos would be on the floor. I'll just take the evidence with me until I look into this fire a bit more. I'm not satisfied with the boy's explanation. Looks like he met more with a bear than a tumble down a stairway."

The ambulance was leaving, so Constable Fleury offered to drive Liberty home to her parent's farm. The dog barked and the officer bent over to look deeply into the dog's eyes. "Okay, Cleo, but if you get one hair on my back seat, you're dog meat." Liberty graciously slipped into the constable's car, and prayed he would not question her before she had time to think more clearly.

Joel said nothing until he was almost into her parent's yard. "You're shaking, Liberty. This one has got to you, eh?"

"It just all happened so quickly...that's all. I was visiting with him...simply paying my respects over his father's death...and then all of a sudden, he's a bloody mess, unconscious in a burning house. It's just unbelievable."

"Yes, that's exactly how I see it...unbelievable," the officer expressed with cynicism. He did not believe for one second that William's slashed arms were caused by a tumble down the staircase.

Joel Fluery was a longtime friend of Liberty's father and was like an uncle to the youth of the district, so she felt nauseated at concealing evidence from him. "I work this evening, so I better get ready. Cleo and I thank you for the ride."

"You want me to drive you to the hospital? You sure you should be working when you're upset like this?"

"No, I'll be fine, just fine. I'm used to handling accidents. You know me...steady as a rock." She stumbled as she stepped out of his police car.

"Aaah, you're just afraid that handsome doctor of yours will think I'm cutting in on his time," Constable Fleury teased, and Liberty shook her finger at him in a scolding manner.

"You're a tease."

The fifty-one year old constable laughed. "You take care now, Missy. Tell Dr. Feddin to call me when McTavish wakes up...Oh, and I'll be wanting you to come into the office for a chat when you get off shift. Make a statement. Okay?"

Liberty nodded and rushed into the house to change into her nurse's uniform. She wanted to be at the hospital the moment William regained consciousness.

Dr. Feddin asked Liberty to watch William's bedside and notify him should the young man awaken when he was elsewhere in the hospital. Liberty waited anxiously, hoping William would soon regain consciousness without anyone else in the room. She wanted to ask a few questions before she confided her entire story to Constable Fleury. The wounds on William's arms were now bound with bandages, along with two broken ribs and the blow to his head. She watched his chest rise and fall with uneven breathing, his ribs obviously causing him discomfort. Every once in awhile his eyes would wince in pain and she wondered if it was from his injuries or from nightmares of the trauma that caused them. Liberty knew from the trashed house and William's beaten body that a battle had taken place. Whoever left William to die in the fire was not a righteous person. But did that make William the better of the two, or was one participant as corrupt as the other? After all, William had worn a gun.

His eyes blinked a few times and then remained open. William turned his face slowly to focus on Liberty as she rose from her chair to walk close to his bedside. "Okay. Before you have half the hospital staff and the police department in here questioning you, what went on back there?"

William attempted to open his mouth and she interrupted

abruptly, "Don't even think of lying to me. I don't have time for that. Falling down the stairs doesn't cut it. Do you honestly think Dr. Feddin doesn't know those are knife wounds? He's no fool...and neither am I."

William's face turned pale and he closed his eyes for a moment, speaking with a somewhat defeated breath, "I pray yer not the welcoming committee at heaven's gate." He gave a few more attempts at breathing normally. "Sometimes it is best to mind your own business."

Liberty would not be dismissed so easily. "Oh! Was that before or after I dragged you out of your burning house?" Her voice commanded the truth. "I saw the trashed house...and the gun you were wearing. You were expecting trouble, and that someone tried to kill you and I want to know why. I haven't told anyone what I know...yet...so you had better make it good and quick before you have half the town in here."

He opened his eyes again, and looked deeply at her. He could see she was not a person easily excused. He would have to satisfy her with a partial explanation or risk her discussing the situation with others. "He didn't try to kill me. He knew you would see the smoke and return before the house burned."

"That's kind of taking a chance, isn't it? I may have decided not to enter the burning house...or succumbed to smoke trying to get you out."

William grimaced, and spoke between painful gasps of air. "Aye! Well, that's...sort of the thrill of it for him. He wants me...'to die a thousand deaths' is how he put it. It's a challenge for him...to see how close he can bring me to death...without me actually dying."

Liberty was horrified. "That's sick!" She glanced towards the door, hopeful that no one else would enter until she heard the entire story.

"No! That's evil," William rephrased in a cold sharp tone,

"and you be best away of it. He doesn't care about you or anyone in his path to get to me. You keep your mouth shut...or you die."

Liberty attempted to question further, "But I..."

"I confided in a lass once...and she's dead," he interrupted sharply. He turned his face away, ending all conversation.

Liberty's face turned ashen white, and she swallowed the words she was going to ask. A fearful shiver passed over her shoulders. She reached over and rang the alarm button to inform the doctor William had regained consciousness.

With no proof of crime or charges laid by William, the police had nothing to go on except William's frail story of falling down the stairs and knocking over a candle. As there was no insurance on William's house, not even an insurance company had reason to investigate the cause of the fire. However, Constable Fleury pursued an investigation for police records and for his own peace of mind. He was unable to gather much information. The house had totally burned with no clues as to its cause. The slashes on William's arms were obviously knife wounds, but no charges of assault could be laid if William did not lay them or admit to them. William's tale of falling down the stairs while carrying a tray of glasses could be neither proven nor disproved. The blood on the photos was the only hope for discovering a possible second participant in the fire.

The one truth that surfaced was William's last name, due to a valid driver's license in his wallet. According to Constable Fluery's investigation, William Casson did exist once upon a time in the small Irish village of Kliborn, but William's whereabouts had been unknown to Kliborn since his early teenhood. The police in Kliborn expressed to Constable Fluery that there was some belief in William being responsible for the suicide of fifteen year old, Elizabeth McGillvary. Nothing could be proven but people had their suspicions.

"Tony and William were a pair of recluses," the Kliborn Police Chief explained to Joel Fluery. "Sometimes, people never saw them for months at a time. William never attended regular school because Tony issued a doctor's confirmation stating that the lad had a mental disability, so the authorities just let them be. The only time anyone saw William was when Tony would whip the lad all the way home for sneaking off to see that McGillvary lass. Tony always carried a long twisted cane and a narrow strap of horse harness. He'd poke that lad ahead of him with the cane and strap him raw all the way home...but William never seemed to learn...He'd always get caught with Elizabeth again."

"And no one in the town tried to help the boy?" Constable Fluery expressed critically.

"Children on the poor side of town often fall through the cracks," the Kliborn officer resolved. "You've got to understand. Poor folk have enough heartache and headache in their own households. They don't need any more...Besides, McTavish was a crusty old cuss and nary a one wanted to ruffle his feathers."

"Even if he was abusing a child?"

"Folks excuse their lack of involvement by excusing the situation. It happens all the time. For the village of Kliborn, they turned their eyes the other way because McTavish put a roof over the orphan's head, and that was more than anyone else was willing to do."

Constable Fleury wasn't pleased. "I imagine the boy figured a whipped hide was a poor tradeoff for a roof over his head."

"Aye. No doubt, but best ye be not feeling too sorry for the lad. William was no saint. Folks often figured he was just the extended hand of the elder. Spat in the eye of Angus Reid, he did, when Angus tried to take Elizabeth away from him and send her home one day...and look what happened to her in the end. You keep William Casson. We nay want him back here...or that miserable old McTavish."

Joel gathered what information he could from the Kliborn Police Chief before visiting William in the hospital. He first questioned William on his whereabouts for the past eighteen years.

William simply responded, "Am I charged with something?"
"Not at the moment," the Constable said, letting William know the situation was open for further investigation.

"Then my past is my own," William snapped, refusing to cooperate.

Constable Fluery remained firmly at the end of William's hospital bed. Joel was Metis, the son of a French father and Ojibwa mother. He had his father's strength of character and his mother's gift of insight. He clearly realized there was nothing mentally deficient in the mind behind William's intelligent eyes of ice. Having learned of William's abuse as a child, Joel was slightly more tolerant of William's indignation than he normally would be. "What was your relationship to Elizabeth McGillvary?"

William's head snapped up and his mouth dropped open. He had no idea that Constable Fluery had researched him so thoroughly, and it frightened him to have his past traced back to Elizabeth. Using his correct name on his passport and license was a planned trail for Dwight Fox to follow, but William had not planned to involve locals in his trap to catch Fox.

"We...were childhood friends."

"Seems some folk in Kliborn feel she might have been assisted in her decision to jump off a bridge," Constable Fluery stated, resting his hands on his hips in attempt to appear more intimidating, so that William would perhaps be more generous with his information.

William looked away and stared out the window. It still pained him to speak of Elizabeth. He couldn't think of a thing to say.

"What's your take on it?" the Constable asked again, giving William ample chance to tell his side of the story.

"We were just kids. Not much we could do...but make plans."

"Plans to what?"

"Run away."

"What's with her taking a dive instead?"

William's words were little more than a mumble. "I don't know. Maybe...maybe someone scared her." His eyes were still diverted out the window.

"Why would someone want to do that?"

William inhaled deeply, fearing his answers were getting too close to a dangerous secret. "That's my business."

Constable Fleury's patience was thinning. "Well, if Tony was alive today, I'd say it was your business, but at this moment, Tony McTavish is dead. Elizabeth McGillvary is dead. You were a hair's breath away from being dead, and Liberty almost dead with you." The Constable's voice rose with a frustrated pitch. "Does this not seem to form a pattern to you? You were beaten and left to burn...in my community...which I watch over like a hawk. So don't you '*my business*' me."

William looked him square in the eye and spoke with such conviction that the hair raised at the back of Constable Fluery's neck. "Look! I have lived in hell a long time...lived it...breathed it ...drank it...lost a friend because of it...until I am now hell itself. If you get sucked into the abyss of my life, you will never get out...Leave me be...Sir."

Joel Fluery looked at William without moving or saying a word for a good three minutes. There was something risky about the young man that made Joel feel like he was hovering over the entrance to a black hole. One could hover above the situation for only so long before it would suck you into unknown territory, and Joel was a person who liked to know where he was going. He backed away for the time being. He nodded to William, accepting the young man's request to leave him alone, because the constable felt William spoke honestly from some dark place that he didn't want to go, at least not today. The officer walked out of the hospital room without asking another question.

Liberty tried to distance herself from the case, explaining she had dragged William Casson from the fire and that was her only part in the affair. However, Constable Fluery had known Liberty since the day she was born and he knew her never to be one so close-mouthed about a situation such as this. Even her police statement was short and not made with the kind of thorough documentation that Liberty was noted for in her hospital reports. He sensed she was involved deeper than she admitted, and decided to guard her from a distance, waiting for clues to surface.

Several weeks passed, and Dr. Feddin approached William for dismissal from the hospital. Dr. Feddin was a thin young man with dark hair buzzed off in a short crop. He stood slightly taller than William and wore a small beard which added maturity to his otherwise youthful face. "I'm sorry, but Milford's hospital is closed for a month with renovations, and this hospital is full to capacity with the overflow. I'm going to have to move outpatients like yourself to other locations. There's the Red Sea Hotel on the west end of Glenfield if you want to rent a room by the month. You're going to be in some discomfort for a bit yet, and you need to stay quiet. I also want you to check into the office here regularly for awhile, have the bandages on your arms changed, your concussion and ribs checked and so on."

William mumbled low, "I'll be alright. Can I get a ride from someone out to the farm to get my truck?"

Liberty spoke up quickly. "I'm off shift in 5 minutes. It's on my way home." William attempted to refuse her offer, but she continued, "First, I'll pick you up some new clothing. Your others are with the police. Do you have a credit card, cash or something?"

William hesitated, not wanting this intimidating lady to become involved any further. However, Dr. Gary Feddin made the mistake of making the decision for William, and that was like striking a match on flint. "You'll not take him home," Gary foolishly ordered without Liberty's consent. "I'll arrange for someone else." His outright mistrust of William created instant rivalry between the two young men.

"There's cash in my wallet," William said to Liberty in deliberate opposition to Gary's rejection. William gestured towards his wallet in the hospital cabinet drawer.

Dr. Feddin threw Liberty a disapproving scowl, but she ignored it, picked up William's wallet and left the room.

Gary glared at William like a rooster about to jump into a sparing ring. "She's important to me," Gary warned. "You cause one hair on her head to be out of place, and you'll be a very sorry soul."

William only acknowledged with silence.

"Even small towns have teeth," the doctor warned again, and left to follow Liberty down the hallway and into the staff lounge.

"I don't want you taking him anywhere," Gary expressed angrily again. "There's something unsafe about this guy. He's messed up with something bad. I'll get a couple guys to take him out to his place."

"I'm just giving him a ride home, that's all." Liberty argued. "It's on my way. If he had wanted to hurt me, he could have done so the first day I visited him."

"The nurses say he hasn't said two words in weeks, other than thank you for a meal. He's bad news. You know there's been talk lately of suspected grow-operations around. He could be a drug dealer. Who knows what him and Tony McTavish were doing down in that valley all by themselves. They certainly weren't making money out of farming."

"Now you're accusing him of something you have no proof of. That's not like you, Gary. You know there wasn't a drop of drugs in him when we brought him in."

The doctor cupped his forehead in his hands. "Drugs or not, someone wants him dead." He paced up and down. "Okay, I give up. Drop him off at his place...but have your cell phone in your pocket...I mean it. And call me the second you drop him off. If I don't hear from you by 5:15, I'm sending Joel."

"I promise." She leaned forward and kissed Gary on the cheek before hustling away.

It wasn't until Liberty was in her car, driving to the store to pick up a shirt and jeans for William, that the severity of the matter hit her. Gary was right about William being messed up in something wicked. Nobody knew it better than herself. She couldn't explain why she wanted to help him. Maybe his first reluctance to let her get involved was a small omen that he was a good man in a lot of trouble.

She stopped at the store and opened his wallet in the car before going in. She noted his photo on the driver's license, and her eyebrows arched. Perhaps he was the only person on earth who took a good photograph for his driver's license. She opened the bill compartment and her eyes grew large at the high denomination of bills in his wallet. She feathered through two thousand dollars. The fear of it being drug money instantly crossed her mind, now that Gary had mentioned the possibility. She ran her fingers through her hair in dilemma. She stuffed the money back in the wallet, and approached the store to purchase the clothing, praying that she wasn't going to be using drug money, counterfeit bills, or something of the like. When she went to pay for the clothing, she took out her own wallet instead, and paid for the purchase personally, just in case his money was faulty.

"Good guess!'" William expressed to Liberty as he walked out of the hospital bathroom, wearing the jeans and buttoning up a denim shirt.

"Well, I cheated. I asked the store keeper. You're about the same size."

"Have the police said anything to you about returning my photographs?" He attempted to tuck the shirt into his new pair of jeans, but having bound ribs, he winced and let the shirt drop loose.   "They're checking them for someone else's DNA," Liberty advised.

"What good will that do? I haven't pressed charges against anyone." He attempted to bend over and tie the shoe laces on his running shoes, but being that it was too painful to bend, he left the laces trailing.

Liberty finally took pity on him and dropped on one knee to tie his shoe laces. She opened the door into the hospital hallway. "Well, you don't know Constable Fluery. I would say that should you wind up dead on another occasion...which is a high probability in your case...then at least he will have a lead with DNA tests." She pointed to a wheelchair at the entrance to his room. "Hospital policy that you get a ride to the door."

William ignored the wheelchair and proceeded down the hallway on foot. She ran to catch up. "Yes, I think I do know Constable Fluery; a very...perceptive man." William expressed with satisfaction. "Anyhow, he won't find any other blood."

"What makes you so sure of that?" Liberty asked, as they walked briskly down the short corridor to the exit door.

He politely held the door open for her. "Devils don't have any."

A ghostly shiver crept through Liberty. "You say things like that, and you'll be finding another ride." Liberty unlocked her car door and they slipped into the front seat. "Before I drop you off at your farm, I'll stop at the Red Sea so you can book a room."

Liberty stood about ten paces back from William who attempted to register at the front desk of the Red Sea Hotel. Mrs. Ruston, the hotel owner refused to let William rent a room. Gossip spreads fast in a little town. "I'm sorry. We want no trouble. How do we know that someone might come back and try to kill you again, and burn the whole hotel down with everyone in it?"

"It was an accident. I knocked over a candle when I fell down the stairs," William tried to explain.

"Yes, well, I'm sorry, young man. We can't take chances, now can we?" She closed her registration book with a decisive snap that would make a turtle jealous, and slipped it below the counter. Mrs. Ruston wore her grey hair in a tight curly perm, and Liberty mused that should William upset her further, her curls would pop off her head like bed-springs.

William did not argue his case further and Liberty did not want to appear involved, so she remained by the door and said nothing to help him.

"Now what?" Liberty sighed, as they reentered the car.

"I'll stay overnight in the barn, and get a room in Milford tomorrow. Right now, I'd like to get out to the farm before it rains. I see a storm rolling in."

Liberty dropped him off at the farm, but hesitated in leaving the yard. She could see shingles missing on the old barn roof and knew in about fifteen minutes, rain would be pouring through the roof like water through a food strainer. Liberty took out her cell and called Gary as she had promised. Then, for a few minutes, she deliberated on whether or not she should leave William to a fate of drowning. A light rain began to bounce droplets off the hood of the car.

She watched William grab a spade from an old shed and quickly dig up a plastic bag at the edge of the rocky fence line near the barn. "Lord," she prayed aloud, "I hope it's not a body."

He returned to her car, holding a black garbage bag in one hand and supporting his injured ribs with the other. He smacked the garbage bag on the hood of her car, pulled a thick briefcase from the bag and then approached her open side window. Rain dripped off his unruly hair and down his face. "Why are you still here?"

"Because, unless you plan to spend the night sitting upright in your old truck, which I doubt your broken ribs are going to enjoy, you will drown in that barn." A flash and boom of thunder rocked the yard. "Get in."

With briefcase in hand, William leaped into the car just as a downpour varnished the car. "Sorry. I'm wet," he apologized, as the rain from his clothes absorbed into the car seat.

"What's in the briefcase?" Liberty questioned. She half expected him to open it and a case of illegal money to fall out.

"Passports...passport," he corrected quickly. "...computer, that sort of thing."

"Gun?"

"That too." At least he was honest.

Liberty looked across the yard at the pile of ashes that had once been his house, and sighed. "So, is it safe to take you home to my parent's place for the night or will our house wind up looking like that?"

"Do you have other guard dogs?"

"You mean other than Cleo?"

"Yes, other than Cleo. I hate to put my life in the hands of a dog who can be bribed with pie." He did not crack a smile.

Liberty turned the key in the ignition and drove out of the yard towards the east.

Liberty had confided partly to her mother and father that she thought William Casson was a good man in a lot of trouble. She hadn't mentioned seeing his gun or repeated his story about the revengeful person who was trying to kill him a thousand times. Most of what her parents knew was from local gossip. The community believed someone had attacked William and tried to burn the evidence with a fire. No one believed William's tale of the staircase accident, and it appeared William didn't care whether they believed it or not, so long as he could avoid an investigation. The local coffee shop was filled with possible motifs, everything from painting William as a gang member to a drug grower. The one thing all morning coffee patrons agreed on was that William Casson was a target for somebody and they didn't want to wind up in the cross-fire.

Liberty and William dashed into the front door of her parent's farm house, drenched from the rain on route from the car. Liberty's mother met the pair with an armful of towels. They dried their hair and then stood on the doormat, their clothes dripping into the braided mat. Liberty introduced her guest with a small, almost apologetic voice. "This is William."

Her father stood in the archway between the kitchen and living room, and Liberty could see him inhale a long deep breath, as if he knew the gates of hell had just been opened and it was too late to close them. "Welcome, son...I'll get you a change of clothes." He turned and disappeared.

Donna Enn's eyes were fearfully wide, but she smiled as she gathered the wet towels from their arms. "We'll get you dried off, then I'll fix you both something hot to eat." She hustled off with Liberty, leaving William to deal with Mike Enn's scrutiny.

Mike returned with a pair of his sweat pants and a T-shirt. "Figured it was almost bedtime anyway. Your clothes should be dry by the time you leave in the morning." It was an order more than a statement. William understood the underlying meaning, but he did not fault the man for protecting his family.

"I'll get a room in Milford tomorrow. The Red Sea wasn't ..." He put his hand to his forehead and slightly wavered. Mike Enns reached out to steady William on his feet. "I...I'm just a bit tired...that's all. Not used to being on my feet. Can I lay down a bit?" William rested his hand on the wall to strengthen his stance.

Mike led him to a spare bedroom just off the kitchen entrance and handed him sweat pants and a t-shirt. Once alone, William instinctively checked the window lock and pulled the blinds down. He placed his briefcase on the bed, opened it and withdrew a small pistol to slip beneath his pillow. He changed from his wet clothing into warm, dry night clothes and fairly collapsed on the bed. He was asleep in minutes, perhaps the only complete sleep, other than unconsciousness, that he had had since Tony's death.

Liberty returned, dressed in a long nightgown and knocked on his bedroom door to summon him to lunch. No answer came, and she gingerly opened the door, fearful at his silence. In sleep, William did not look like a dangerous man. His handsome young face camouflaged the scars beneath the surface, and hid the callus on his trigger finger. Liberty scooped up his wet clothing and called for the dog. "Come here, Cleo." The Border Collie entered the bedroom with a lazy saunter.

"Stay!" she ordered, and the dog jumped up on the bed beside William. Liberty smiled with a satisfying grin. "Good dog! I'm sure he's going to love that." She closed the door quietly and let William sleep.

Liberty returned to the kitchen where hot chocolate and warm cinnamon buns greeted her. "I'll put his clothes in the laundry room. He's sound asleep. Best leave him be."

"Perhaps you should have thought of that before you brought him home," her father suggested.

Liberty's shoulders collapsed in dismay. "I'm so sorry, Dad and Mom," she apologized with deep emotion. "I just...didn't know what to do with him. The Red Sea wouldn't take him in. I was simply dropping him off at his farm when the rain came down. He's in real bad trouble. I guess you know that...I don't know why it should concern me, but it does...I have this strange feeling about him...like if we let him die, the devil wins big."

"Gracious, Liberty. You'll have us building a fort around him." Her mother poured Liberty a cup of hot chocolate, overflowing the cup from nervousness. She grabbed a cloth to wipe up the spill. "Here, give me those wet clothes and you sit down and drink this." Liberty handed William's wet clothes to her mother and sat down at the table with weariness.

"What's the story with him?" her father asked solemnly. "Joel was here and mentioned he's worried you're messed up in something with this guy. I told him he was crazy. Was I right or wrong?"

Liberty sucked in a deep breath and let it out slowly. Lying to her father was not something she could easily do. "I really don't know what I'm messed up in," she confessed honestly. "William won't say much. I saved his life. Maybe I messed that up for someone." Liberty shrugged her shoulders in bewilderment. "Obviously, someone wants him dead...or to suffer, but I don't know why. He told me to keep my mouth shut...for my own safety. I figure if he was worried about my safety, he can't be completely bad."

Donna looked at her husband anxiously. "More than likely concerned about his own secrecy. I really don't like the sound of all this. Whatever he's into, he's in pretty deep for someone to want to beat and then burn him to death." She slipped a sweater around her daughter's shoulders for extra warmth.

Mike Enns studied his daughter's face. "You have a good feeling about him, eh!"

Liberty nodded.

Mike looked at his wife. "Never heard her say that before...Kind of hate to see the devil win big."

"I have a feeling too," her mother expressed with a worried frown on her forehead. "If we try to help him, one of us could be the next victim."

Liberty's father turned to his daughter with a serious face. "You realize your mother is right, don't you?"

Liberty nodded in agreement, a mixture of fear and compassion on her face. "You're right, Mom. I know it's dangerous to have him here. I'll ask him to leave in the morning."

"He can stay a few days until he's stronger," her mother relented. "In the meantime, I hope you realize I expect locked doors and alarms and the whole bit. I'm not going to have my house burned down, or find him cut in quarters on my kitchen floor."

"Sounds like your young man has found himself a guardian angel for a few days," Mike laughed.

"I think Cleo has already accepted that job," Liberty smiled, grateful that Cleo's ears and eyes were extra keen.

Donna reached across the table and took their hands in each of her own. "Be careful! And I don't mean only with whoever is after William. We don't know who William is either. We may have just made a pact to protect the devil."

One day turned into days, and days into weeks, and after Dr. Feddin's initial explosion upon learning of William's new temporary residence, things settled down for a little while. As for the two photos, tests revealed William's DNA, the Fire Chief's, and another's DNA unknown to any data-base, as of yet. Constable Fluery was not satisfied and did not return the photographs to William.

William revealed no more details to the Enns family about his situation, feeling it safer for them if they knew little of the hell that would eventually catch up to him. However, Joel had passed on William's early history to the family, so they at least knew his mysterious and troublesome beginnings. They all agreed that something unnatural had gone on behind closed doors in the McTavish household in Ireland.

William was a quiet guest, speaking little, and moving about the house like a soft breeze. He accepted few favors, repaying each back in his own fashion. Although he was secretive, when you live in the same household for a while, truths have a way of unraveling about you, whether you intend them to or not. The Enns family soon discovered William was either naturally talented or explicitly trained at about everything he worked at. Donna referred to him as having the Midas touch when it came to fixing broken furniture, plumbing, wiring, computers, vehicles or anything in his path. Mike had never worked with a more skilled tradesperson.

They also noted that he could speak with skilled knowledge on any subject from economics to political and foreign affairs, should they ask his opinion. His insight on subjects spoke volumes of what wisdom lie hidden inside him, and that mystified the Enns family.

"I swear, he could say he was Einstein and nobody would question it," Liberty voiced one night after William had gone to bed. "Constable Fluery said he was never schooled because Tony issued a document saying he was mentally incapable, but there is nothing unschooled about him. He is obviously well educated and well trained, so he must have had tutors...but why would Tony McTavish have William taught in secret? What would be the purpose of that?"

"Every day, he shocks me," Mike expressed in bewilderment. "There is something very spooky about that guy."

Donna Enns spoke in hushed tones, so William couldn't hear from his bedroom. "I heard him speak in German to the dog today. My mother spoke German, so I know. He didn't know I overheard him calling Cleo a nice dog, but he patted Cleo's head and said, *"Nett Hund! Nett Hundi!"* An Irishman speaking German to a dog? Now what's with that?"

"I don't think we have a clue who he really is," Mike acknowledged with caution, "and I've got a feeling whoever tried to kill him is out there and not finished with this matter, and William knows it. I can see it in his eyes. He's always watching out the window. Have you noticed?"

"Yes!" Liberty nodded in agreement. "I don't think a fly passes by that he doesn't see."

"I honestly think one of these mornings, we'll wake up and he'll be gone, "Mike expressed somewhat sadly. "Might be the best thing...but I'll miss him a bit. He doesn't say much, but I swear his head is an entire encyclopedia if you ever want to know anything."

Liberty felt a strange tightness in her chest, sad at the thought of William disappearing. However, she realized dangerous winds were blowing over their household and that it was only a matter of time before William's attacker returned. She would never forgive herself if something bad happened to her family because of her bringing him into their home. She knew William shouldn't stay.

William usually drove alone in his truck to his doctor appointments. He did not want anyone to view him as being dependent on the Enns family. However, on one occasion, Liberty accompanied him on route to his appointment, and asked him to stop at the Chinese Dragon Cafe' to pick up a take-out order for dinner. When she exited the Cafe', she found William beside the truck, conversing in fluent Chinese with Jo Wong. They stopped speaking immediately when she approached. Jo Wong bowed politely to her and hustled quickly back into the cafe'.

Liberty plunked herself down on the truck seat beside William in a frustrated fashion. Why should she be surprised to find out he could speak Chinese. Her mother had overheard him speak German. "Okay, why and how do you know Chinese?" She was agitated that once again an unexplainable mystery surrounded William.

"Oh, I just know a few words."

Liberty knew it to be a modest lie. She had overheard him speak quite fluently in Chinese to Jo Wong. "What were you talking about?"

"He asked if you were my girl now? Seems like we are the latest gossip since Jed Chapter's multi engagements to four ladies in town."

"Oh great", she sighed. "Just what I need. I hope Gary hasn't heard this gossip?"

William smiled with great devilish pleasure. "According to Jo Wong, Dr. Feddin tried to bribe Mrs. Ruston with paying double the hotel fare if she would let me have a room at the Red Sea...to get me out of your house." He chuckled out loud. "...but Mrs. Ruston told him she'd rather house a sea of rats."

Liberty rolled her eyes. "Well, get your appointment over with at the hospital and then let's get out of town before anyone else sees us together...and take that grin off your face." It was maybe the first time she had ever seen William truly relax enough to laugh, and it bothered her that he had such a charming smile. "How do you and Jo Wong know each other so well?"

"Seat partners on an airplane last year, coming back from China."

Liberty looked at him crossly. It annoyed her that he was an endless sea of surprises. Now she discovered he had traveled to the far ends of the earth. "China! What were you doing in China?"

"Designing a security system for a government agency. That's all."

"That's all? You design security systems for governments?" Liberty's voice rose in pitch. She thought he never left the farm.

"Sometimes. Sometimes I do the opposite."

"What do you mean by that?"

"Sometimes I'm the one they're building the security against."

Liberty was even more frustrated by his vague answers. "Who on earth are you?"

He leaned over and whispered in her ear. "A chameleon can be anything." His warm breath traveled down Liberty's neck and she couldn't breathe for a moment, half out of fear and half out of feeling his closeness.

After a lengthy silence, Liberty gained the courage to ask, "Have you ever killed someone on one of your assignments?" She recalled the hidden gun under his jacket when she first met him, and it had always bothered her as to whether he used the gun for protection or for force.

"Yes!"

She was terribly disappointed. "Are you a spy?" She hoped to find some reasoning for his actions; some thread of goodness that she could forgive his failings for.

"Sometimes."

"For the good side, I hope."

"Well...I suppose each side would consider themselves the good side, now wouldn't they?" Seeing her frustrated face, he added, "It would be easy if all choices were simply black or white, or good or evil, but I'm afraid what I do falls into a grey area some of the time."

"I had kind of hoped you were one of the good guys," she said. "I'm rather disappointed." She moved farther away from him on the truck seat to show her disapproval.

He accepted her rebuttal, and parked the truck in front of the doctor's office. He left her in the truck while he attended his appointment, which gave Liberty time to digest what he had said. Liberty decided she shouldn't judge him until she knew all the facts. She knew all about that 'grey area' because that's exactly where she was sitting at this moment by not telling Constable Fluery all the details that she knew about the fire and William's attacker. Liberty decided to reserve her final opinion until she learned the entire truth of his situation. When William returned to the truck, he noticed that she had slid herself back to her original spot on the seat beside him. She kept her face aimed forward, for she was still angry at his secrecy. However, he interpreted her moving back closer to him as somewhat of a truce.

September breezes cooled the air and Liberty invited William to accompany her for a walk through their pasture. Every year at this time, she picked goldenrod plumes for her grandparents' grave. There had been an early frost, so the leaves on the trees were beginning to change to autumn hues along the tree-lined meadow. Liberty stretched her arms out, trying to catch aspen leaves as they filtered down in shades of tangerine and melon. "Goldenrod was my grandmother's favorite," she said cheerfully. "She said it reminded her of sunshine. Would you like me to pick extra for Tony's grave?"

"He wasn't much for flowers."

"What did he like?" Liberty snapped off several golden spikes and laid them in her basket.

He thought for a moment. "He liked...creating monsters."

"That's a strange thing to say about your deceased step-father."
For a moment, Liberty thought him callous to speak of Tony McTavish in such fashion.

William folded his arms and looked skyward. "What defines a father? Is he someone who sees that you are clothed and fed, or someone who lets you climb into his bed at night when you're afraid of the lightning and thunder?"

"Probably both," Liberty said apprehensively. "Sounds like you weren't cared for very well."

"Oh, I was cared for. Tony guarded me with life and limb until the day he died...just not with an ounce of compassion."

Liberty reached out and took his hand gently, looking up into his face with soft emerald eyes. "I'm sorry you missed out on a loving family life. Every child should have that. Just make sure you don't pass Tony's failings on."

William looked down at her slender fingers wrapped gently about his hand like a bandage. He drew her hand up to the open throat of his shirt, where she could feel his heartbeat travel down her arm. "And how do I begin to do that, sweet lass?"

Liberty stuttered nervously, aware of his perspiration against her hand as it lay tucked against his chest. In a shy, tiny voice, she suggested, "Per...perhaps you could...forgive him and...put flowers on his grave."

William smiled mischievously back, not letting go of her hand which bound her close to him. "But he doesn't like flowers," he whispered, his blue eyes teasing her.

She stepped back and freed her hand. "Well, I don't care," she snipped haughtily. "He's going to get a sprig of goldenrod anyway." She snapped off an extra flower and slapped it down on top of the others in her basket. Her freckled nose tipped up in the air defiantly.

William chuckled aloud, thinking that for the first time, Tony McTavish would not have his way.

As Liberty turned towards home, her one foot caught in an abandoned gopher hole and she sprawled upon the trail, releasing the basket of hand cut flowers. The basket rolled down the embankment, shooting out arrows of golden spikes at every roll.

William hastened to kneel beside her, and cupped her foot gently in his hand. She winced with pain. "Oooh! It hurts." She closed her eyes and pinched them tight.

William scooped her up into his arms to carry her homeward. "The basket!" she cried out, and reached her one arm out towards the basket, which had rolled half-way down the river bank beside the trail. William gave her a stern, forget-it glare, so she relented, "Okay! I guess we will get it later...but I am rather peeved to think Tony McTavish had the final say in putting flowers on his grave."

William froze, sat her back down on the ground and walked down the embankment to retrieve the basket. As he walked back up the incline, he gathered her cut flowers and filled her basket once again with the luminous goldenrods. He handed her the basket and swung her into his arms to carry her home. There was no way he was going to let Tony win this argument.

"I know it's a big favor to ask," Donna begged of William, "but she can't drive with her foot and she's too proud to ask you for help. Her father and I are invited to Agnes and Bart's 50th Anniversary and Gary is swamped at the hospital, and there just isn't anyone else who can spare three days to drive her to and from a nurse's convention in Saskatoon."

"Three days?" William was surprised that they would trust him alone with their daughter for that long.

"It will take one day each driving there and back, and one day for the convention. Hotel reservations are already made for guests of the convention. Would you considerate it?" Donna pleaded, having full trust in the young man's integrity, even if she was apprehensive of what he did for a career.

William nodded. "Anything for you...and your chocolate chip cookies."

She hugged him. "I'll make a fresh batch right now. You can take some with you in the morning. I'll tell Liberty. She was so disappointed not to go."

"I can tell her," William smiled mischievously, knowing Liberty would at first refuse and then submit to the torture of traveling with him. It wasn't that the two of them disliked each other. On the contrary, they were attracted to each other and knew they should not be.

The morning the couple left for Saskatoon was pleasant with a haze over the sun and warm westerly winds. Liberty had not informed Gary of whom her driver was going to be for this trip, hoping she could return before telling Gary, and that his displeasure would be somehow less if she was back before he found out.

William turned on the car radio because he knew silence would soon bring forth a flurry of questions from Liberty, which he did not want to answer.

An hour was about as long as Liberty could constrain herself without talking. She reached forward and turned off the radio. "Thank you for taking me to this convention."

He nodded in acknowledgement, hoping she would turn the radio back on, but she did not.

"Tell me about Elizabeth?" she asked, and William felt his stomach tie in one giant knot. He should have known Liberty would question him about Elizabeth sooner or later.

"What do you want to know?" He knew her inquisitive mind would not let him rest until she knew every detail.

"You told me once that you confided in her and that's why she died. Do you think someone pushed her off the bridge?"

"I don't know...but then I don't know if my parents died accidently in a car crash either. I always thought it strange how I wound up with Tony. I've searched for answers half my life...until after a while, I closed the door in order to find some peace of mind. I don't think Elizabeth felt trapped enough to jump off a bridge. She didn't frighten easily. She took all those chances meeting me over the years, so why would she jump off a bridge when we were about to escape?" His jaw tightened and

Liberty could see the despair of feeling powerless on his face. "The only reason I can think of for anyone wanting to murder her would be to keep me with Tony. Whether that was Tony's personal doing, fate, or the hand of someone else in the Agency, I don't know. The truth, unfortunately, died with Tony...unless Strauz spills it someday."

"Who's Strauz?" she asked apprehensively.

"No one you want to know." Silence fell for a few moments. Then William continued with renewed strength in his voice. "Life is not a fairy tale where we always solve the crime in the end, or where the good guy always wins, or understand why bad things happen to good people. Sometimes we just have to accept what life throws our way, and deal with it."

"I guess that's where faith comes in," Liberty said quietly, not knowing any other way to cope with unexplainable dark times.

He glanced at her, realizing there was a sweet innocence to Liberty's life that he never remembered having. He smiled slightly, thinking that one never really knows yourself until you have been tested. Sometimes under pressure, the meek turned out to be the strongest and the strongest crumble. He had a feeling gentle Liberty would be solid as a rock if she needed to be.

Nothing more was said for a long time. William thought and hoped she had at last abandoned the subject on Elizabeth, so relaxed a bit on the car seat, but the lull in conversation was only temporary while Liberty watched the sunset blossom and fade into dusk.

"What was Elizabeth like?" Liberty suddenly questioned further. She realized that Elizabeth would always have a corner of William's heart, and that was good, for she felt it only right that his friend should have a special place where she would be treasured and not forgotten.

William's eyes grew distant, as if he could see Elizabeth in the shadows of the road before him. "She had long black curly hair that almost touched her knees. Often, we would lay in the grass when we were children, and she would untie the ribbons from her hair and spread her hair out like a soft blanket for us to lay on. She would listen to my problems about Tony, and we would make plans to run away when we were older. Her parents were from the richer side of town and they didn't want her associating with the likes of me. The first day we met was in the long grass by the river. She had lost a kitten and I helped her find it. We stayed secret friends for seven years."

William suddenly gave a small laugh, remembering a past incident. "She made great escape plans. When we were eight, she packed a week's food for us, threw our coats in the river to make it look like we'd fallen in the river, and then we hid in an old abandoned culvert under Mill's Road, planning to stay there until they stopped looking for us, then sneak out in the night and run away."

"What happened?" Liberty asked with keen interest.

"After one day, we got a heavy rain that filled the culvert and we were forced to either flee or drown. Of course, we got caught. I think I still have the scars of Tony's cane on my backside from that episode." William's eyes gradually saddened and he glanced out the side window so she could not see the pain on his face. "When we were fifteen, we decided we were old enough to try our escape again. The next thing I knew the authorities were at our door, informing Tony that Elizabeth had jumped off the bridge and drowned, and they blamed me for causing her to do it. My whole world died right then and there." A sorrowful silence fell over the car. Then William added, " I think that's the only time Tony showed me an ounce of compassion...He brought me a cup of tea."

The thought of Tony's small gesture of compassion meaning so much to William broke Liberty's heart. Tears filled her eyes. She looked down at her foot in a cast and visioned Elizabeth with her long black curly hair strewn across the grass like a dark, wavy sea. "Maybe someday if you have a little daughter, you could call her Elizabeth."

William turned and looked into Liberty's kind, gentle face. Freckles sprinkled across her nose like cinnamon on an apple pie, and his heart came alive again. "That's probably the nicest thing anyone ever suggested to me."

Liberty smiled shyly at him and turned the radio back on. She would give him peace now and stop asking questions.

Suddenly, he was singing to the music on the radio, and it did not surprise her that his voice had perfect pitch and harmony.

Upon arriving at the pre-registered hotel, the couple met with a problem in overnight plans. "I'm sorry," the receptionist explained. "All rooms are filled. The rooms were pre-booked as dual occupancy, and you and your accompaniment are in Room 352." She slid the card locks to the room across the counter towards Liberty.

"But...but he's just my driver...because of my foot." Liberty held her cast out so the receptionist could easily see it from over the counter. "I was supposed to be roomed with another nurse coming to the convention."

The receptionist slowly eyed William from head to toe with raised eyebrows. "Honey," she said to Liberty, "if my roommate looked like that, I wouldn't be complaining."

A slight smile tipped William's lips. When Liberty turned to glare at him, he diverted his gaze to the spinning ceiling fan, and spoke in a half whisper, "Your call."

"I'm just too tired to stand here on one foot and argue," Liberty sighed, and grabbed her crutches, which she had leaned against the counter. She limped towards the elevator while William following behind with the overnight cases.

Once in the room, Liberty turned to him and warned, "One word to anyone about this arrangement, and I'll have you shot."

He mumbled something about, "Not if Fox gets to me first."

She was relieved that there were two beds, and sat down on the edge of one quilt with her head lowered, shoulders drooping and arms limp at her sides in exhaustion.

"Would you like me to order in some supper? You look too tired to go out." He handed her a hotel menu from the cabinet. "My treat...I snore sometimes...so people have told me. It will be sort of my pre-payment to compensate for that."

Liberty laughed in spite of herself. "In that case, I'll order chicken fingers, a tossed salad, small dish of maple walnut ice-cream, a pitcher of black coffee...and ear-plugs."

With their evening meal over, Liberty called the desk for an early wake-up call, and decided to retire to bed. Although she was tired, she lay awake a long time in bed, conscious of William lying in the other bed beside her. He had been a complete gentleman, never once acting in any manner that was not appropriate. She wondered if he was fighting the same human magnetism that she felt towards him. He was an honorable man, and that trait only made him appear more attractive to her.

When William began to snore slightly, Liberty turned on the nightlight by her bed and playfully tossed a pillow at him, not realizing that his instincts had been trained like a soldier.

In a flash, he rose with a revolver in his hand, the gun having been previously slipped beneath his pillow. Liberty's mouth dropped open in shock and for several moments the two of them sat half upright in their beds, staring wide-eyed at each other like two deer caught in a headlight. Gradually, he lowered the gun, uncocked the trigger, and slipped the gun back under his pillow.

"You...you were snoring," she said in a very low, shaky whisper. She turned the light off and lay her head back down on her pillow. She had forgotten who he was and the danger he was in, but obviously he had not forgotten.

He lay back down on his pillow and heaved a few deep breaths. "I'm sorry about the gun," he whispered into the stillness, realizing that he had frightened her, "...but not the snoring. I already compensated you for that."

"Sometimes I forget who you are," Liberty answered back into the darkness.

"That's alright. Sometimes...when I'm with you...I forget who I am too." William sat up on the edge of his bed and walked to the window. He opened the curtains to look down and check the parking lot where they had parked their car. The lights of the city silhouetted him against the window. He wore only pajama bottoms, so his bare shoulders and biceps caught the shimmer of city lights.

Liberty thought how beautiful he was, standing still like a bronze statue in the darkness with only the city lights permitted to touch him.

He closed the curtains again and returned to bed, adjusting his pillow so the revolver was easily retrieved, should the slightest shadow cross the room.

Liberty noted he did not snore the rest of the night, nor the night of their second stay at the hotel before returning home. She wondered if it was because he lay awake on guard all night, or if she was simply getting used to his sleeping habits.

Dr. Gary Feddin was Liberty's life-long friend, a relationship which simply never changed over time. Liberty couldn't remember Gary ever asking her to be his girlfriend. He just became it, like people who find a penny and keep it in their pocket until it belongs to them. Being both in the medical field, they had a common understanding of its demands, and so when planned dates and activities were cancelled or late, the two of them adjusted to the situations with little complaint. Their relationship was one of harmony and mutual understanding. Gary had never asked Liberty to marry him, and Liberty had never pressed him to ask. They were in a comfort zone, much to the disappointment of the community who loved to wed their young people and fill the churches and school yards with the next generation.

It was on such an occasion that Gary was late picking Liberty up for the Annual October Ball in Glenfield. Liberty had purchased a long slender gown of russet satin and lace. She pulled her hair up and clipped it with ivory, pearled combs, letting a fall of natural curls frame her face. She sighed. She wished the makeup would stay on those darn freckles on her nose.

She finally accepted the person who looked back at her in the mirror, and came down the stairs. William was sitting on the sofa in the living room, reading a newspaper when she descended the stairs. He rose as she approached, his eyes drinking in every curve of her body in the hugging russet satin. The material reflected attractive flames in her auburn hair and seemed an appropriate color for the October season.

"How beautiful you look," he said with quiet admiration, noticing how green her eyes suddenly seemed.

"Thank you, kind sir," she said with a little curtsy. "But my freckles will soon escape this camouflage. The moment I dance, a bead of perspiration will tip my nose and alas, Cinderella will be cinder girl again."

William smiled quietly." Well...perhaps we should give it a trial run, shall we?" He leaned over and pressed the CD player. Music began and he reached out his hand, inviting her to dance with him. "I'm not the Prince, but perhaps the Magician will do."

Liberty's heartbeat quickened as she accepted his hand and was lead to the open floor of the living room. His one arm circled around her back and gently drew her close to his chest. His cheek brushed her hair as they swayed to the rhythm, his lead keeping her in perfect unison with his step. Gradually they became one with the music and one with each other. She didn't remember when the music stopped, just that William's lips were suddenly touching her neck below her ear. She pushed back in fright.

"I'm sorry," he apologized quickly in earnest. "I forgot my place."

Liberty backed up several paces, turned and ran up the stairs, more frightened of her own feelings than William's slight touch of a kiss on her neck. Half way up the stairs, she gathered control of herself and returned slowly down the staircase, one delayed step at a time.

William was standing at the fireplace, staring down into the unlit logs with great despair. Liberty approached him from behind. "I'm sorry," she apologized. "I overreacted. You just frightened me for a moment."

He spun around to face her, responding with great regret in his voice, "No! You had a right to be upset. I know my place. You are not my lass."

Liberty fidgeted a little and raised a finger to brush a curl from her forehead. "You told me once that a chameleon could be anything, and I had a feeling you were talking about yourself at the time. I'm not sure who I'm dealing with under your coat of many colors."

"Well," William said somewhat sadly, his Irish accent suddenly becoming more distinct, "there be roses in everyone, ifin ye ever came close enough to see them."

Liberty stared at him, ever so tempted to step closer and ask if she was close enough.

The kitchen door opened and Gary yelled, "I'm here. Are you ready to go? Dustin Tilley held me up with a broken wrist. The kid put on a Superman cape and jumped off the garden shed...We'll be late if we don't get going."

"I'm ready," Liberty called to him, and then turned to William. "It's funny. I know every rose and thorn there is to know about Gary Feddin, but I have a feeling I would never be able to say that about you."

William gave a sly little grin. "Your freckles are showing."

Liberty's hands rose to cover her nose in dismay. She frantically rustled in her purse to find a compact to powder her nose. Upon looking in the compact mirror, she discovered her makeup was in perfect order and not a freckle to be seen. "You are NOT a nice person," she retaliated, and hurried off to meet Gary at the kitchen door.

William smiled as he watched her heels clip saucily across the hardwood floor. He kind of liked her freckles.

Cool autumn rain forced chores inside the barn, which gave Liberty the opportunity to discuss her older sister with William. "Felicity is needing help to raise her daughter," Liberty explained, "so they'll be arriving here next week from the coast. Felicity was widowed a number of years ago, leaving her with a daughter to raise. It's becoming increasingly difficult for her, as she wishes to pursue a career in order to give them a better life, but doesn't want to leave Heidi with caretakers so often." Liberty flipped a pail over and used it as a seat to sit on. "My sister was always adventurous. You would like her. She hopes to be a lawyer someday."

Liberty's eyes directed out the barn door at the rain, which screened the entrance like a waterfall. "Felicity got married right out of high school and about the only thing Andy owned was a backpack and a motorcycle...which was fine for the two of them for a while. They journeyed all over Canada and the States, and had their adventures...but sooner or later, one has to put roots down, especially when a child comes along."

William leaned on his pitch fork. "I know the feeling," he said.

Liberty traced a pattern in the dusty barn floor with the toe of her boot. She knew by telling William about Heidi's arrival that she was also informing William he could not stay. It was an awkward and painful moment. "Heidi is nine now, and growing up so fast. Andy had little insurance so Felicity was left with practically no financial support. We've sent money to help, but she's an independent woman." Liberty rose and walked across to the entrance to check the rain clouds. Seeing no break in the rain, she returned to where William casually rested his weight on the fork handle. Liberty sat back down on the over-turned pail. "Felicity fears Heidi is lacking the attention and stability that a child needs. She has asked if we could help raise Heidi here on the farm for a while until she finishes law school in Regina."

William nodded in understanding. "That's as it should be. It's good to have family you can depend on." A touch of sadness ran through him, for he suddenly remembered and missed the security of Tony's watchful eye, even though he had tried so many years to escape the man. "What happened to her husband?"

"Avalanche in the mountains. Andy loved to ski, but his love for adventure lured him into unrestricted areas once too often. Fate caught up to him a few years ago."

William stuck his fork in a bale of hay and sat down on the bale adjacent from her. "I have a feeling I have lived in unrestricted areas most of my life. Fate will probably catch up to me one of these days too." He removed his cap and ran his fingers through light brown hair to brush the fall from his eyes.

"Maybe it's time you changed your fate," Liberty suggested.

"Aah! If only life was that simple. I'm afraid I am buried too deep in the snow to get out now." He kept his eyes lowered and focused on the barn floor. "I try to picture what a normal life would be like sometimes...me walking along with a kid on my shoulders...but that would mean I'd have to find a wife."

Liberty playfully tossed an armful of hay at him. "Yes, having a wife usually comes first, and that won't be easy."

He laughed and shook the hay from his hair. With chores done, they waited at the barn entrance, debating on whether or not to dash to the house in the rain.

"I'll be leaving in a few days," he said to her as they walked briskly to the house to avoid getting wet. "I realize I must be gone before the child gets here. We don't want to endanger her."

Liberty nodded. She was glad that he understood. Putting Heidi in danger was not acceptable. "Will you be back?" she asked sadly, thinking how much she would miss this intriguing young man.

He shrugged his shoulders. "Perhaps...if I can outfox a fox."

Fearing William would soon be gone without a trace, and her family not able to reach him, Liberty planned to find out the Agency's name and address. She was fearful that William's attacker might return. She knew William would not trust to give her such information, but she felt she could be totally trusted with whatever she learned, so could see no wrong in obtaining the name and address any way she could. Liberty lay awake a long time, gathering up the courage to check his briefcase. She was positive the answer had to be in the briefcase for he guarded it so carefully. There was no way she could sneak into his briefcase in the daytime. Her mother had given him a key and his room was always locked.

She rehearsed the plan over in her mind until it seemed a necessary deed. At three o'clock in the morning, she slipped down the stairs, her negligee fluttering like a white moth in the shadows. She knew William should be asleep, having grown accustomed to trusting Cleo as a guardian at night. If not, she would make the excuse that she thought she heard Cleo bark, and had come to check. He would be angry at her for doing so, but not as angry as he would be if he knew the real reason for her being there. It seemed a good plan; a necessary plan.

Liberty spoke softly outside William's bedroom door to alert the dog. She knew Cleo would not bark if he knew it was her opening the door. She slipped silently and carefully inside. Cleo raised his head, but being familiar with Liberty, the dog lay his head back down on William's stomach. William moved slightly and she held her breath until he settled into stillness, and breathed a deep sleep once more. She planned to slip the case out of his room, examine the contents in the privacy of the bathroom and then return it.

Liberty carried a small pen flashlight and flicked it enough to search the room for the briefcase. Gingerly, she slid the closet door open, holding her breath that the sliding doors would not squeak. He had only a few clothes hung in the closet, so she quickly determined the case was not there. She had to leave everything exactly the way it was when she entered, so carefully closed the closet doors again, praying they would not make a sound. She kneeled on one knee and lifted the bed skirt to check under the bed, but the case was not underneath. She thought to herself, "Surely he didn't bury it outside again."

She stood erect and peered around the room. Cleo's eyes followed her but he did not move, as she signaled with her hand for him to 'Stay'. A dresser cabinet stood beside the head of William's bed. The cabinet drawer was just big enough to possibly hold the briefcase. She tiptoed close to where William's head lay asleep on the pillow and prayed he would not open those two, piercing blue eyes. Then she turned her attention to the cabinet and attempted to pull out the drawer. The drawer creaked!

Liberty felt her body flung through the air and nailed to the floor with such a thud that her head snapped back and hit the floor like a hammer. The penlight lay beside her stunned head, spinning in a circle and casting out beams like a disco light. William lay frozen on top of her, a gun to her temple, as the light barely distinguished her face to him.

In defense of Liberty, Cleo grabbed William's arm in his teeth. "Easy boy," William soothed the dog, and Cleo released his hold and lay down beside the two on the floor, a small concerned whine escaping his mouth. William slowly uncocked the gun and lay it on the floor beside her head. Liberty had not moved and lay petrified in fear, her breasts rising and falling deeply with panic.

He lifted himself off her and sat upright, his face distraught in the knowledge that he had almost killed her. "You foolish, foolish lass. Damn! I nearly shot your head clean off. I'd think you'd know better after throwing the pillow at me in Saskatoon while I was sleeping."

Liberty lay still on the floor, her hair sprayed out like sunrays about her face. Her delicate white negligee barely concealed the shapely body beneath its thin fabric, and William's anger subsided as he looked at her trembling and frightened form beside him. He reached over and lifted her into a sitting position. "Are you hurt?"

She lowered her head in deep shame and could not look up at him. "A bit dizzy." She reached her hand up to rub the back of her head. "I'm sorry," came out of her lips in a feeble whisper. "I wanted to look in your briefcase and find out who you worked for...in case we needed you."

"Don't you think I would have told you that, if it had been in your best interest to know?" he said angrily. "Did you think I would just leave and not have someone watch over you?"

Liberty started to cry in the aftermath of being frightened half to death. Tears rolled down her cheeks, falling onto her bosom. William reached out and brushed them away with the slightest touch of the back of his hand. Their eyes locked and slowly they leaned into each other until their lips touched slightly. Their eyes closed, and for a moment, they forgot the world around them and the danger of their situation. Then William withdrew and shook his head, for he knew having such feelings were not in the best interest for either of them. He looked at her in the shadows with only the small penlight to give them a sense of surroundings.

"You must not try to locate me ever again," William ordered, his face solemn. "You might lead Fox to the Agency or to me, and that would be your death sentence."

"Why can't your Agency stop Fox if they are so powerful?"

"Dr. Dwight Fox is an elusive mastermind. He is someone who blames me for the death of his children."

"You killed his children?" Great dismay crossed her face that he could be involved in such a deed.

"Indirectly. My part was to befriend Fox, work with him as a fellow scientist until I gained his confidence and learned his plans for developing a plant contaminant, which would produce deadly seed in the first germination. He intended to sell this poisonous strain of grain to terrorists who would then distribute the seed to their enemies. I was to learn the location of his secret laboratory and files, then pass this information on to the Agency. I had no idea that they planned to blow him off the face of the earth after they received my information. I seldom know what the other end of the Agency follows up with. Fox was a divorced man and no one realized it was his weekend for the kids. The bomb blew his residence into the sea...and his kids with it. He alone escaped."

Liberty shook her head in dismay. "That is horrible. No wonder he wants you to die a thousand deaths."

"Yes, well, he intended to cause the deaths of thousands of other children, but that never seems to cross the mind of a terrorist."

"What are you going to do?"

"That is not something you want to know." William scrambled to his feet and lifted her from the floor. "Now you must promise me that what I have told you stays with you and your parents. Speak of it to no one else. Not Joel Fluery. Not Gary. Not even your sister. The less that know about me, the better, for all your sakes. The only reason I am explaining this to you is so you understand why you must never attempt to locate me again. Promise me."

He gave her a stern shake to reinforce the importance of what he was saying. "Your life will be worthless if either Fox or the Agency think you can influence me." He looked straight into her eyes with fire. "Dwight Fox would dangle your life in front of me as bait, and the Agency would snuff you out like a candle to prevent it. Understand?"

Liberty trembled in his grasp and bit her lip to keep from collapsing into a flood of tears.

William's face had become unusually cold and he frightened her. "They own me. Do you understand?"

She nodded her head in agreement, squinting her eyes to hold back tears. "Then take care of yourself, William Casson," she spoke hushed in the moonlight. "If you're still alive...come home for Christmas."

"Home?"

"Yes, home." She turned and climbed the stairs without looking back. She was sure she would crumble to dust if she looked back.

In the morning, he was gone.

William straightened his tie and took a deep breath before raising his hand to knock on the Captain's door. He never knew what Strauz was thinking. The Captain could curse you and praise you in the same breath, and you would walk away not exactly knowing where you stood with him.

A voice boomed, "Come in, C-3. I've been expecting you."

William approached the solid oak desk with strong, sturdy strides. He had been summoned before he was barely off a long flight and did not feel like discussing business at this time. He stood silently, eyes focused on the veins in the wooden desktop, thinking that the desk was solid and formidable like the POLLU Agency and the man in charge of it.

The Captain did not rise to greet William. In doing so, he would have appeared on equal footing, which did not fit in with the lecture he was about to give William. "So Fox got to you again," Captain Strauz said in a voice that showed more displeasure than concern. "You've depended on Tony guarding your back far too long. Made you sloppy."

William said nothing for there was a partial truth to the Captain's reprimand. Tony had always arranged William's security, and after years of expected protection, he felt naked without it.

The Captain continued, "Sorry to lose Tony. Have you tied up all the loose ends in Glenfield?"

"Not quite. There's the land to sell." William had not attempted to sell the land because the valley gave him a sense of roots somewhere, even if he never set foot on it again.

"You should have done that months ago."

"It's wasteland...a hard sell."

"Then leave it to charity or something...You have any other ties there?"

William answered, "No!" almost too quickly and the Captain raised an eyebrow at William's immediate response.

Captain Strauz didn't argue the point but he took note of William's overly defensive attitude. His eyes narrowed as he scrutinized William's face. Then he moved forward with his discussion. "We had a mission waiting for you, but this Fox character is a drop of poison in our system. I'm afraid to chance the mission now using you. Fox might foul it up. Too bad! We received a good tip on how to squeeze information out of Sinclair Molley."

William glanced up at the Captain in interest, for as much as William felt forced into the life of being a chameleon, he did take a conscientious interest in his missions, which was why he excelled at carrying them out. Strauz continued, "We were going to have you pose as a priest at St. Michael's. Molley works for the Greenway Chemical Company and is responsible for their chemical waste disposal. We'd like to know where he's dumping, as there seems to be a huge discrepancy as to where half of it is going."

"What's being a priest got to do with that?" William questioned, still standing before the Captain's desk.

"Molley is a man with a guilty conscience, not an altogether evil man, but someone who asked for too many favors along his road to success, and now they've called in the favors. According to a close source, he regularly goes into retreat at St. Michael's after every unethical decision he is forced to make. If you befriended him at St. Michael's, he may loosen his tongue."

William frowned in opposition to the idea. "I don't think I'm exactly priest material."

"Yes, well, I agree to that! Anyway, we have to shelve the mission for the time being. Our first priority is to eliminate Fox before we make you anything, much less a priest...and I'm not sure if your loving nature as a man-of-the-cloth would shine through enough to attract Sinclair Molley's trust."

William scowled back. He was not in a 'loving nature' this day.

The Captain leaned forward and waved for William to sit down adjacent from him in an overstuffed leather armchair that William always disliked. William obeyed without a word but sat on the edge of the seat, not wanting to be smothered by the pumped armrests and quilted back of the chair. The Captain scoffed, "You look like a lion about to spring from its lair. Relax! You are safer here than any place on earth." William gave him another cool glare, for putting an animal in a cage and then calling him safe did not impress the young man.

The Captain leaned back in his chair and observed the valuable chameleon before him. He had known William since childhood, from the first day Tony McTavish brought him in to study with the best of the best tutors. Tony had flown William back and forth from Ireland to Germany and to other countries around the world many times, so that William might learn their customs and languages fluently. Tony had chosen his chameleon well. The young man was extremely intelligent and put his skills into action with far more authenticity than the handful of others chosen for the Agency...but William had one defect. He was intelligently defiant. The Agency had always been successful in rehabilitating subjects into working willingly with the Agency's worthy cause. Such was not the case with William.

The POLLU Agency used a handful of chameleons trained from childhood to extract information from any source in any country. Choosing a child and then training him or her as a chameleon took years of careful input. They needed super skills to pull off their roles with perfection. William was their most skilled chameleon. Unfortunately for the Agency, William Casson was not content with his calling. He continued to be a wildcard that they could never fully trust.

POLLU was an agency that worked secretly to end criminal activities related to pollution and contamination of land, water and atmosphere. POLLU worked endlessly in areas where conventional methods failed. Some governments paid well to use the agency, but because POLLU's methods were sometimes unprincipled, no government would admit to using them. The survival of the planet was POLLU's ultimate goal. They felt humankind would survive if earth survived. If sacrifices had to be made, it was for the good of the whole. William disagreed with that philosophy. He never lost his fire to revolt on such matters. For William, one life was as valuable as a million, for was it not said that God's eye was even on the sparrow. When an innocent was sacrificed, William drew back farther from the Agency, feeling they had no right to decide who would live and who would die.

Captain Strauz tolerated this defiance in William because Chameleon-3 was a genius who could speak eleven languages by the time he was fifteen, and now at thirty-three, he was trained to slip into any position in any country as smooth as a silk glove. He was valuable beyond words. One of the Captain's greatest regrets would be if he had to eliminate William for the good of the cause, should William put the Agency at risk. For that reason, POLLU kept a close eye on Chameleon-3. It was now extremely frustrating to the agency to have scientist, Dr.

Dwight Fox enter the scene and foil their security on William.

"How are you feeling?" the Captain finally asked.

"I was wondering if you were going to ask," William said sarcastically. "My head pounds when I talk too much."

Captain Strauz's iron face broke into a rare smile, for he knew William never spoke '*too much*'. "Well, I guess then we have nothing to worry about." He looked at the tired young man in front of him. "Get some rest, Wil. It's been a long plane ride from Canada to Germany. I'll see you tomorrow...6 o'clock sharp."

William looked up at him warily. It was the first time he remembered the Captain calling him anything other than C-3. Code names were used to lessen any personal connection in decision making. William was not sure if his spoken name was a mere slip by the Captain, or if the Captain was letting him know in his own way that William meant more to him than just a valuable asset. William hardly doubted that Strauz meant the later, so he nodded his head in acknowledgement and exited the room.

The Captain tapped his fingers on the desk in deep thought and concern. The world needed William Casson. The Captain leaned back in his chair and rubbed his chin thoughtfully. Captain Strauz was a psychiatrist by former trade. He could see William was in somewhat of a depressed state, but not over Tony's death. Chameleon-3 had left something behind. In one way, this displeased the Captain, as it was Agency policy to cut all ties once a mission was completed. But in another way, the Captain thought perhaps C-3's tie could be used to the Agency's advantage in catching Dwight Fox. Maybe sending William back to Glenfield was the best trap of all.

Felicity and her nine year old daughter, Heidi arrived at the Enns farm with little more than their car full of boxes and suitcases.

Felicity had thought about the situation for over a year. It was not a hasty decision on her part. She had weighed the pros and cons a million times, knowing she would miss special moments in Heidi's life by not having her daughter with her, but also knowing Heidi was alone too much with caregivers in Vancouver while she was working. It was not easy being a single mother. Heidi needed family.

With Heidi tucked snuggly in her new bed in Liberty's bedroom, Felicity sat at the kitchen table, itching to question her sister on this mysterious young man who seemed to have an unusual grip on the family. Felicity thought it strange that her family still held a spare bedroom open for the absent William Casson. "Okay," she grabbed Liberty's arm and plunked her sister down at the table beside her. "I can't wait any longer. Tell me about this guy. All I know is someone beat him up and you saved him from a fire, and he wound up here for several months."

Liberty proceeded to explain, leaving out the dangerous details of her last conversation with William.

"Ooooh, I love a mystery," Felicity's voice bubbled with excitement. "I wonder who tried to kill him and why. Do you think he's in with drug dealers or something? Well, if he is, I'm glad he's gone. We sure don't want him around Heidi."

"He would never harm Heidi." Liberty was quick to defend William. "He's a good person...just in a bit of a mess."

"I should say!" Felicity exclaimed. "Not all of us have enemies trying to burn us to death. I just don't understand why you are still keeping a room spare for him. I think I'd nail the door shut to keep him out."

"He might...pop in to say hello...sometime." Liberty's reasoning sounded foolish because she could not explain all the details to her sister. William had warned her to keep silent.

Felicity folded her arms and proceeded to investigate Liberty's face with eagle-eye scrutiny. "Okay. Is he handsome?"

Liberty shrugged her shoulders. "I never noticed." She grabbed a cup and poured herself some coffee so she didn't have to make eye contact with Felicity.

Felicity broke out in a knowledgeable grin. "Don't tell me the serene life of Liberty Enns has suddenly been jolted with electricity." Felicity had always been of the opinion that someday Liberty and Gary's passive relationship would simply fade into a forever friendship and never make it to the altar. "What's Gary think of the guy?"

"Pretty much the same as Mrs. Ruston at the Red Sea Hotel," Liberty answered, and gave her hair a toss as if to indicate that she didn't really care what others thought of William.

"And what's that?" Felicity asked with amusement on her face.

"They both think he's a rat." Both sisters broke into uncontrollable laughter and Donna Enns entered the kitchen to see what the joke was about.

Felicity's face was bright with the warm glow of coming home and sharing family gossip, which she had not had the pleasure of doing in a long time. She reached out and slipped her arm around her mother's waist. "You know what, Mom, I like this mysterious William and I haven't even met him yet." The three burst into more laughter. Stories about William's talents and strange past filled the hours deep into the night.

Felicity stayed three weeks, helping her daughter adjust to new surroundings and school. She purchased a second-hand piano and had it delivered to the Enns household on the day she had to leave. "Now you can continue your lessons," she said to Heidi, "and each time I visit, you can play for me."

Heidi adjusted quickly, as her mother promised to visit often and correspond daily by computer. The child adored the piano, the horses in the barn and friendly Cleo, who still sat in front of William's bedroom door every night, waiting for his return. It was a far better life for Heidi than being watched by caregivers in a small apartment in Vancouver.

"How come Cleo likes William so much?" Heidi asked, eyeing the dog that appeared like a permanent rug in front of William's bedroom door.

Mike Enns laughed. "Cleo doesn't want to admit he's one of the unemployed, but you and I know he's guarding an empty room. Just don't let Cleo know that you know that."

Heidi took note of the conversations that her grandparents had with Liberty about William. She never let on that she was listening, but she eventually built an image in her mind of a super hero who was off somewhere fighting the bad guys. Heidi had not had a brother in her life or a father figure that she could remember very well, and so she built a fantasy about William, secretly writing down all the conversations that she overheard about him.

The adults tried to keep any talk of Dwight Fox secret from Heidi and her mother, so as not to frighten them, but Heidi was thirsty for information for her diary. Regarding herself a secret spy, Heidi made it a game to listen around corners and behind doors. Learning information on William became an obsession with her, and something to do when she was missing her mother. Every night she pulled the blanket over her head, turned the flashlight on under the sheet, and relayed whatever she had overheard into her diary.

Today I heard Gramma and Grampa talking outside with Constable Fleury. He said he investigated William's photogragh, and one picture was of his parents who died in a car crash. The other was of William with Tony McTavish. He said one of the DNAs on the photographs belonged to Tony, only Tony was actually Anthony Antonios who once worked for the Italian mafia long ago. He said Tony was reported killed about twenty-five years ago, and likely that was when he left for Ireland..--Agent Heidi

Winter fell upon the Canadian prairies and as was the custom in the Enns household, preparations for Christmas began. Although Liberty never said a word about William returning, Heidi could feel her aunt's anticipation in the way Liberty hummed Irish tunes around the house instead of Christmas carols. Every time a car drove into the yard, Heidi noticed her aunt hurry to the window, and then heave a sigh as if the visitor was not whom she hoped for. At night, Heidi continued to write her observations in her diary.

Liberty told Gramma that she asked William to come home for

Christmas, but Gramma said he likely wouldn't come because of me. I don't know why it matters about me being here. Aunt Liberty even told me that if William came home, she would ask him to look for kittens in the loft of the barn for me, because she heard some kitten sounds up there last week.

I also heard Auntie Liberty crying tonight. She didn't know I heard her, because they didn't see me when I came down stairs for a cup of water. Gramma told Liberty that a lady shouldn't cry when a man asks her to marry him, but Liberty said Gary didn't ask. He just said he was giving her an engagement ring for Christmas. That's all! Gramma said it shouldn't be a surprise to Liberty that he was going to give her a ring, but Liberty said even if it wasn't a surprise, a lady should be asked. She said she didn't tell Gary yes or no because he never asked for yes or no. Jeepers, I don't understand all that engagement stuff.

Anyhow, I hope Liberty marries William, not Dr. Feddin. Until tomorrow--Agent Heidi

Liberty and Heidi hustled in and out of the department stores, shopping for Christmas gifts. On one occasion, Heidi asked, "What are you getting William?"

Liberty turned to her with flushed cheeks. "He likely won't come. He has a lot of work to take care of."

Heidi tucked her mitten around Liberty's hand with encouragement. "There's still two days. He'll make it. What do you think I could give him? I want him to like me."

"He would love you no matter what. How about...if he comes...you can play him a piece on your piano...that new one that you've been practicing. I think he likes music...I heard him sing once... actually, exceptionally well...and we danced once..." Liberty's eyes got a faraway look in them, and a soft smile of remembrance cupped her lips.

"I guess there's nothing he can't do, huh!"

Liberty sighed. "Well, sometimes it seems that way...but even a chameleon can't do everything. Besides, doing good is more important than being good at something. Remember that!"

"A chameleon is a lizard that changes colors with his surroundings. Why did you call William a chameleon?"

Liberty put her hand to her mouth. "Oh, did I? I meant to say com...a complicated man like William can't do everything."

Heidi changed the subject, but she did not forget the chameleon reference and decided to write about it in her diary. "Are you going to marry Dr. Feddin?" she blurted out, knowing that Gary had said he was giving Liberty an engagement ring for Christmas.

"He hasn't asked me yet."

Heidi's forehead wrinkled in a confused frown, but she didn't want her aunt to know she had overheard Liberty's conversation with her grandmother. "A mood ring is sort of like a chameleon, isn't it?" Heidi asked, taking off her mitten to show Liberty a smooth, ever-changing stone in her ring. "My friend in Vancouver gave it to me when I left. You never know what color it's going to be. Is William like that?"

"Very much so," Liberty said somewhat wistfully. "You just never know about William."

That night, Heidi slipped beneath the sheet covers, turned on her flashlight and wrote:

Today, Aunt Liberty called William a chameleon. She pretended she made a mistake, but I know she didn't. I think chameleon must be a code name or something. I bet it's William's secret agent name. I wish I could check things in William's room, but Gramma keeps the room locked all the time. William must have something secret in there. Otherwise, why would she lock it? Maybe that is why Cleo guards the door. I am going to watch where Gramma keeps the key.--

Heidi was not of the impression that she was doing anything wrong by pretending to be a secret agent gathering information. Even spying on her grandmother to find the location of the key seemed a game to her. She finally came to the conclusion that her grandmother must keep the key to William's bedroom in her purse, but she had been told by her mother that it was improper to go through someone else's purse. Twice, Heidi lifted the purse from the kitchen counter where her grandmother always left it, but twice, Heidi returned the purse to its position and did not open it. She decided she would just have to get the key in a different manner. She looked at Cleo and sadly expressed, "It's not easy doing the right thing, Cleo. Mom wouldn't like it if I went into someone else's purse without permission...but I have another idea."

"I think I hear the window open in William's room," she suddenly declared late that evening. Heidi didn't realize the fright she would cause by the false statement. She thought she would simply discover where her grandmother kept the key to William's bedroom door. But suddenly, Liberty grabbed the child and held her close, while Mike Enns hurried and unlocked the gun case and took out his rifle. He waved for Heidi, Liberty and Donna to go upstairs. Heidi looked back as she climbed the stairs, too frightened to admit that her lie had caused this false panic.

Heidi saw her grandfather remove a photo from the wall, and slip the key off a nail. Then he approached the bedroom with his rifle, unlocked the door and flung it wide. Her grandmother put her hands over her face and started to shake in fear that gunfire would explode. Heidi began to cry, not for herself but because she had frightened her grandmother. Heidi ran and threw her arms around Donna.

Mike Enns came out of the bedroom and yelled, "Coast clear! Window locked! Come on down. All clear!" The women came down stairs with Heidi clinging tightly to her grandmother's nightgown.

"I'm sorry. I'm sorry," Heidi cried over and over.

"It's okay," her grandmother soothed. "It was just a false alarm."

"But it's like the boy who cried wolf when it wasn't true, and then when the wolf really came, nobody came to help." Heidi was well aware of how a lie can have consequences.

"Trust me!" Mike Enns assured his granddaughter, not realizing she had deliberately lied about the open window. "No wolf will get through these doors with me and Cleo." He ruffled Cleo's head and gave her a big grin. "Did you notice that Cleo never barked? He knew all was okay. Besides, this was good...It was a trial run...like a fire drill at your school. Good practice. Now you best get some sleep and stop blaming yourself."

But Heidi did blame herself. She was too distressed to hide under her sheets while writing in her diary this night. She pulled her diary from behind the dresser, sat on top of her quilt and wrote:

Tonight I told a terrible lie and I scared Gramma real bad and I will be sorry forever and ever. I said I heard the window open in William's room, but that wasn't true. I just wanted to find out where Gramma kept the key to William's room. They thought someone bad had broken into the house. Grampa even got out his gun. I'm afraid to tell them why I told the lie because maybe they will think I am trouble to look after and maybe they will get caretakers to look after me like in Vancouver. I won't try to go in William's room again, even though I know where the key is now. I feel too bad about scaring Gramma.- Agent Heidi

Heidi slipped the diary back behind the dresser mirror, and climbed into her bed, which was adjacent from Liberty's larger bed in the same room. After a few moments, she slid back out of bed and kneeled on the mat to say a prayer. "I'm sorry I told a lie, Jesus. I really am. Tell Santa I'm sorry...Amen." It couldn't hurt to cover both bases.

Being on the second floor of the two-story house, Heidi's bedroom window faced the dark woods behind the house, and was above the roof to the back veranda. It was possible, should anyone want to crawl up the lattice on the sides of the veranda, to set foot upon the veranda roof, and have access to both Liberty's bedroom and her parent's master bedroom windows. Mike Enns had considered it a good fire escape. Should anyone have to flee through the windows, they could use the roof to dismount to the ground. No thought had ever been that someone in this quiet countryside might also use the veranda roof for wrong doings.

Outside the window, the snow fell, covering all traces of the coming and going of footprints. A dark shadow moved slightly outside Heidi's window, cloaked in a black hood and overcoat, which camouflaged his form into the night. Through the window, the creature had witnessed the child writing in a diary and seen where she replaced it. Knowing the truths that a diary might contain, Dwight Fox was satisfied with his discovery this night, and like a snake, he slithered down the lattice and made his way back into the woods.

Heidi heard the slight crunching of snow outside her bedroom window. Her eyes grew wild with fear and she slowly pulled the blanket over her head. She thought to cry out, but maybe the sound was just caused by a squirrel or fallen branch. She had cried wolf once before tonight when it was a lie. Now hearing something outside her bedroom window was the truth, but she was too afraid to alert the family twice, in case it was another false alarm. So Heidi curled up in a little ball and lay shaking under her blankets, and didn't say a word.

The freshly fallen snow erased any visible sign that someone had been there. Fox felt confident in his allusiveness, but unknown to him, his scent remained under the feather dusting of snow, and left a trail that a keen nose could follow.

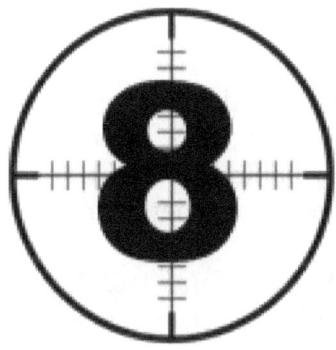

It was Christmas Eve, and the Enns household bustled in preparation for Christmas celebrations and for Felicity's arrival. Heidi practiced her piano piece over and over so it would be perfect for her mother. Then she made sure she hung a spray of mistletoe in the archway to the living room, secretly hoping to capture William and her Aunt Liberty beneath it.

Mike carried in extra logs for the fire, commenting that Cleo must have caught the Christmas spirit too because he was acting like an excited pup out in the snow behind the house. "I swear he tracked a rabbit clear to the river near old Martin's hunting shack before I could call him back."

Heidi choked on a shortbread cookie, and Liberty quickly handed her a glass of water. Heidi was thinking that a rabbit couldn't climb onto the roof of the veranda outside her bedroom window. "Maybe it was a squirrel, Grampa."

Mike screwed his face up to disagree and shook his head. "A squirrel wouldn't run that far. He'd climb a tree." Then he broke into a big mischievous grin. "Maybe it was Santa Claus." He gave her a teasing wink, but Heidi didn't smile. She knew it wasn't Santa Claus outside her bedroom window.

With preparations ready for Felicity's arrival, the family climbed into the car to attend church services in Glenfield. "I left the front door unlocked, so Felicity can let herself in," Donna Enns informed the rest of the family. "She should be here within the hour."

"Don't do that," Heidi protested strongly. "It's not safe to do that." Her eyes were wide with fear, and her breathing became rapid with panic, for Heidi had not forgotten the crunching of footsteps outside her bedroom window.

Donna reached out and laid her hand tenderly upon Heidi's cheek. "What has frightened you like this?" Donna's eyes searched the other faces for an explanation to Heidi's frightful condition. "Did we scare you with the gun the other night?"

"Someone could get into the house," Heidi cried. "He could hide...maybe in a closet or something. You have to lock the door."

Mike's face turned dark and serious. This was not normal behavior for a nine year old child, and yet the child was right. They were beginning to let down their guard against William's attacker. "Tell you what we'll do, sweetheart. Grampa will stay home with Cleo, and I'll read the Bible right in my old arm chair. I'll guard the fort. How about that?"

Heidi broke out in a wide relieved smile and wiped the tears from her eyes. "That would be better. And don't worry, Grampa. William will be home any minute and then things will be okay."

The three adults exchanged a knowing look. Things were rarely okay when William showed up at the door.

Dr. Feddin was waiting for the Enns family outside the church, and approached their group to greet them warmly. He reached out and took Liberty's hand and proceeded to walk towards the church entrance, as was their usual custom. A glum expression clouded Heidi's face. She knew Dr. Feddin planned to give Aunt Liberty an engagement ring tonight. Heidi feared he might give it to her right after church services. She wanted to make sure Gary had no time to be alone with Liberty. She ran forward and tugged at Gary's jacket sleeve. "Can you come to our place after church? Grandmother cooked all this yummy food, and my Mom should be there by the time we get back."

Dr. Feddin stopped and kneeled down so that he was eye-level with Heidi's anxious face. He was touched that the child should give him such a kind invitation. "I would be delighted to come, especially to see your mother. Did you know Felicity and I used to be good fishing buddies...but she caught all the fish? I lost all my hooks in the tree branches."

Heidi sighed, "Ya, well, don't worry about it. It's better to be good than to be good at things...Not all of us can be like William."

Gary Feddin's shoulders drooped in dismay. He sighed deeply and straightened up tall. "Another William fan, I see...and she hasn't even met him yet. How many does that make now in the Enns household?"

Liberty lowered her face in slight embarrassment. Donna laughed politely and hustled all into church before they were late for the service.

Dwight Fox watched the car leave from behind the slightly opened door of the wood shed. He wasn't pleased to see Mike Enns exit the car and return to the house, but at least the dog followed him inside. He tapped the blade of a knife in his gloved hand. The dog going inside was one less messy job he thought he would have to do. He dared not let the dog bark at him while he climbed the back veranda tonight, or decide to follow him afterwards.

With most of the household gone, Fox climbed onto the veranda roof at the back of the house. He was skilled at opening locked windows and doors, and found little problem to slip his blade between the window casings and slide the lock free. Not

81

wanting to leave a snowy trail in the room, he sat on the edge of the opened window and removed his shoes. He knew exactly where the diary was located, as he had watched Heidi replace it behind her dresser mirror. With hasty hands, he whipped the diary out and read her writings about William. His face was expressionless, cold and long ago drained of any emotion other than hate. He had once had a daughter Heidi's age, but William and his agency had taken her and his young son away from him forever.

It was time that William felt the sting of his revenge again. Let William Casson watch shadows until fate took his life. Let him wake in the night, sweating from the horror of dreams, as he did, seeing his house explode in front of his eyes, searching for his children though the smoke and floating ruins in the sea.

Fox replaced the diary and slipped out the window. The snow was still falling and he felt confident that his tracks would soon be covered. He did not, however, take a direct walk into the woods, but detoured through the barn and out buildings, should the dog try to follow his scent again the next day. He planned to dispose of the dog if it tried to track him to the cabin again. An idea came to Fox as he passed through the barn. He remembered a passage from Heidi's diary and his evil eyes drifted towards the loft in the barn where kittens lay.

Fox entered the back door to old Martin's hunting cabin. Carefully, he covered all windows so no ray of light could escape from the cabin. He had chosen Martin's cabin, not only because of its secluded and abandoned location at this time of the year, but because the cabin was connected to electricity and allowed him to plug in an electric heater for warmth. He dared not use the wood stove and create chimney smoke. He withdrew a bottle of whiskey, slab of bologna meat and a loaf of bread from the refrigerator and sat down at the rustic table for his Christmas Eve meal. He had been working for an hour in the loft of the barn and was ready for a rest. Memories of past celebrations did not enter his mind. He drank and ate in great celebration of what was yet to be. He tipped the whiskey bottle and let the spirits burn his throat with satisfaction. It was going to be a great Christmas!

Two cars wound their way into the Enns farmyard. Liberty and Gary returned in one car, with Mrs. Enns and Heidi in the other. They had barely settled into the house, when a third car pulled into the yard.

Heidi had her snow boots on and was out the door in a flash to greet her mother returning from Regina. With many hugs and kisses, Felicity followed Heidi back into the house, and embraced her parents and sister. Then Felicity saw Dr. Gary Feddin, standing quietly by the kitchen cupboards, watching the family reunite. "You still hanging around here?" she said in a teasing manner." I haven't seen you for years. You're looking good."

"I like the cooking...and you're looking good yourself," he kidded back.

"Well, make yourself useful, Doc. Please help me carry in my luggage and presents from the car." He obliged and followed her out to the car.

Heidi could hear Gary laughing with her mother. "I hope you bought a present for me, if I have to carry in all this loot." Heidi glanced at Liberty, but Liberty seemed preoccupied, looking up at the clock as if time was running out for William to come home.

The evening was warm with laughter and the customary singing of carols and family talk. Not a word was mentioned of William but everyone knew that William was on each person's mind. Heidi grew sleepy and eventually resigned to going to bed, but she insisted that Cleo sleep in her bedroom. "When William comes tonight, make sure you tell him where Cleo is," she insisted, as she climbed the stairs with the dog following close behind. "I'll give Cleo back tomorrow. Okay?"

"William won't mind," Liberty smiled sympathetically, for she realized Heidi was in need of Cleo for security.

"Happy dreams! I'll be up soon," Felicity assured her daughter.

"Time for me to go too," Gary spoke up and rose to his feet.

"You'll come tomorrow for dinner?" Donna asked, knowing Gary always showed up for dinner on Christmas Day unless he had a hospital emergency.

"Wouldn't miss it," he said, kissing her on the cheek. Then he turned to Liberty, whom he noticed was unusually quiet this evening. He had conversed more with Felicity than with Liberty. Gary sensed there was concern for William on everyone's mind. It was not a romantic atmosphere for presenting a ring. To be honest, he wasn't really in the mood himself anymore. He had expected more enthusiasm from Liberty. At least, it was nice to see Felicity again.

There had always been a strange friendship between Gary and Felicity. They never hung out in the same circles in high school. Felicity was more out going and always president of this and that, while Gary was content to sit in the back row and never so much as drop a pencil to bring attention to himself. However, except for occasional teasing, Felicity had always treated him courteously and with respect. At first, Gary thought Felicity's tolerance of him was simply politeness due to him going out with her sister, but after awhile, he realized they had formed their own kind of friendship.

Liberty rose from the sofa and accompanied Gary to the door. Her footsteps slightly dragged on the floor as if she was weary. "Merry Christmas, Gary," Liberty said gently and kissed his lips goodnight. Gary could see the lines of worry on her forehead. He knew her so well.

"If he doesn't come, it doesn't mean he's dea...", Gary left the word dangling, but she knew what he was about to say.

Liberty threw her arms around his neck and gave him a giant hug. Gary was her dearest friend and they could read each other like a book. He knew exactly what she was thinking, exactly what she was fearing.

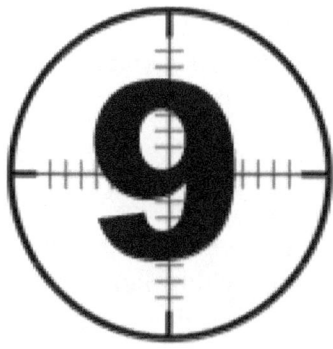

Jo Wong stopped his car and dropped William off a good distance from the Enns' farm house. Christmas Eve was darkened with a cloudy sky that dropped snowflakes upon William's shoulders, but he could still see the twinkle of lights coming from the farmyard. "Want me to wait awhile in case they kick you out?" Jo inquired with a little grin.

William smiled back. He wasn't too confident himself on what kind of reception he might receive. "I want to check the out buildings first and make sure there's nothing suspicious around before I go in," William said. "You go home to your family. Have a good holiday with them, Jo."

"Keep your cell close. I'll be here in a flash if you need me," Jo advised. William nodded back to his POLLU bodyguard.

"Have there been any strangers in town?" William asked as he unloaded his backpack from the trunk of the car.

"Lots of visitors around at Christmas time, but none that seem suspicious." Jo Wong's face showed concern. "But Fox could pose as Santa Claus, for all we would know. You be careful, chameleon. You going to be here long?"

"Strauz wants me to stay until we catch Fox. Otherwise, he'll mess up my next mission. Might be a day or a month. Who knows!"

"I'd say Fox is back in Europe by now." Jo Wong wiped the freshly fallen snow off his windshield with the back of his arm.

William looked towards the farm lights in the distance. It worried him to chance bringing Fox close to anyone other than himself, but he had his orders from Strauz. "Fox is glued to me like a magnet. If I'm here, he'll be here, not in Europe". He patted Jo Wong on the shoulder as if to reassure his bodyguard and friend that he would be alright.

William started walking down the road towards the farmyard and Jo Wong yelled out to him. "Don't you be leaving any broken hearts behind. Liberty's a nice lady."

"I know that," William yelled back. "If there's a broken heart, it'll be mine." William turned and continued down the road.

It was near midnight when William knocked very lightly at the front door. Mike Enns opened the door and they stood staring at each other for a few uneasy moments, neither saying a word. William was thinking it was a long cold walk back to town and maybe he should have asked Jo to wait until he was admitted through the front door. Mike was deciding whether it was wise to let this bundle of trouble back into his house.

Finally, Mike stepped back and beckoned him in. "It's been about two months. How are the ribs and concussion doing?"

"Fine!" William glanced at the table and noticed Mike was preparing a large sandwich for himself. "Mrs. D still got you on a diet?"

"Ssssh." Mike hushed him, as everyone else was in bed and he had slipped into the kitchen to sneak a disallowed, giant sandwich.

"Only if you make me one too," William bargained. He hadn't eaten since getting off the plane and catching a bus to Glenfield.

"You know we have Felicity's daughter staying with us now. You're going to have to play safe with her around." Mike opened the fridge, took out the butter and slapped a layer on a couple slices of Donna's homemade bread for William.

William nodded in understanding, watching Mike heap layer upon layer of meat, tomatoes and lettuce on the bread. He reached out and rescued his sandwich before Mike spread half a jar of mayonnaise on it.

"Her mother's here for a couple weeks too, sleeping with Heidi upstairs. Liberty's with Donna. I've got the sofa, and your room is still waiting for you. Oh, and Heidi said to tell you she's got Cleo for the night. Girl has been acting strange since she thought she heard your bedroom window open the other night. It was a false alarm, but I scared her when I got the rifle out. Now she's pretty skittish."

"Kids shouldn't have to feel unsafe like that. Sorry, I brought my mess into your house. I'll stay tonight but then I'll get a room in Milford for the rest of my stay." William reached forward and poured himself a large glass of milk to go with the sandwich. "I can take the sofa. You have my bedroom," William suggested. "I could sleep anywhere at this moment."

"No!" Mike disagreed, stuffing the rest of his sandwich in his mouth with big gulps before someone came down stairs and caught him eating it. "I don't want to scare the kid if she comes down to peek at presents and sees you lying there. She's never met you before."

"I have a few gifts in my backpack." William gestured towards the backpack that he had carried in. "I'll put them under the tree. Couldn't carry much on the plane."

"I think they'll be just plain happy to see you're still alive, son. We've been worried about you."

"Is Liberty...engaged now?" William held his breath for the awaited answer.

"Nope!" Mike shook his head in bewilderment. "I got wind that he was planning to give her a ring tonight, but nothing happened, so who knows with those two. Their relationship is sort of like warm tea." Then he shook his finger at William in warning. "Don't you ever tell them I said that."

William smiled with relief. His heart felt a huge load lifted, at least for tonight. He put the rest of his sandwich in his mouth and thought that "warm tea" would never describe the feeling that burned inside of him when he thought of Liberty.

"She's not sure about it, you know," Mike said as he walked to the living room, and retrieved the bedroom keys from behind the photograph for William. He looked at William, knowing the handsome and mysterious young man was to blame for Liberty's dilemma. "Too bad, because I'd sure hate to see her give up a good life for one that offers nothing but uncertainties."

William completely understood Mike Enn's concern for his daughter's future, but Strauz had ordered him back here until he trapped Fox. Keeping a casual distance from Liberty wasn't going to be easy.

Heidi was first out of bed on Christmas morning, and pounced playfully on her grandfather, who was sleeping on the couch. Cleo followed her down the stairs and immediately went over to William's door and scratched at the door until William opened it. William's hair was ruffled from sleep and his pajama shirt hung open and unbuttoned.

Heidi had never met William before, and she walked gingerly over to get a good look at the super hero of her life. She stood staring up at him and he at her. "So you're William," she said bluntly. Her two little braids stuck out from the sides of her head like braided straw.

"So you're Heidi," he said with equal bluntness, and put his hands on his hips while he surveyed the perky little elf dressed in a long, red flannelette nightgown in front of him.

"You don't look so tough," she informed him, her brown eyes scanning him from head to toe.

"Neither do you," William wryly replied.

"I don't have to be."

"You better be. All my agents have to be tough."

Heidi put both hands to her lips in awe. She couldn't believe he had just called her his agent. She instantly adored him. Heidi reached out her hand and took his and directed his path to the archway between the living room and kitchen. "Stand here and don't move," she ordered.

Heidi ran to the bottom of the staircase and yelled to the people upstairs. "Come see what Santa brought. Come see!"

Donna, Felicity and Liberty dismounted the stairs, still in their night attire. Liberty approached the tree, adorned with gifts beneath, and then suddenly, saw William standing in the arched doorway where Heidi had posed him. Liberty's auburn hair fell like a crown of unruly ringlets about her face, and she put her hand to her hair, embarrassed that he should see her looking so casual and ruffled. Liberty did not realize how beautifully natural and unspoiled she looked to him.

Heidi grabbed Liberty's hand and dragged her over to William. "Look", she said to William. "You're under the mistletoe. You have to kiss Liberty."

William looked up, surprised to see the mistletoe branch above their heads. Then his eyes twinkled mischievously and he teased, "Well, I think I was standing here first. I think Liberty has to kiss me."

Liberty sucked in a deep breath. "I...can't kiss you. You're...practically...naked." William's unbuttoned night shirt hung apart, baring his chest. His hair was still tousled from sleep and the slight growth of an overnight beard darkened his jawline. She fought to conceal the attraction her whole body felt when she looked at him.

"Oh, for Pete's sake," William exclaimed, and swooped her up like a handful of petals. His arms slipped about her waist, slightly lifting her shirt enough that her bare midriff connected with his, and Liberty gasped as their flesh touched. His lips came down on hers deeply, and then as suddenly as he had swooped her into his arms, he let her go and walked towards the tree. "Let's open presents." His sudden nonchalant actions were a cover-up for the fire of desire that raged through him. He had not meant to let himself be so openly vulnerable to her, especially in front of her whole family.

Liberty stood there with her mouth still open, practically swaying on her feet in the aftermath. Mike and Donna exchanged uneasy glances while Heidi grinned from ear to ear, pleased that her mistletoe plan had worked supremely well. Felicity stood back slightly, trying to form an opinion about this stranger who had obviously just swept her sister's breath away.

"Well, hello, son, and Merry Christmas," Donna Enns finally greeted him, and crossed the room to give him a giant hug. "I'm so glad you're safe." Then she turned to introduce him to Felicity. "This is Liberty's sister, Felicity, and you've met Heidi."

William nodded and smiled. Felicity smiled back, but he noted a small worried frown on her forehead, and he knew she was uncomfortable with the kiss he had just given her sister.

Heidi brought William a present to open. His eyebrows arched in surprise. "For me? I thought all these were just for family." He sat down cross-legged beneath the Christmas tree like a child eager to open a gift. William could never remember opening a gift on Christmas morning after his parents died. He hesitated to remove the ribbon and bow, wanting to savor the moment a bit longer.

"If you married Liberty, you would be family," Heidi blurted out and a silence fell. Only the ticking of the old grandfather clock made a sound.

"Oh Heidi," Liberty whispered in embarrassment, not wanting to upset the child on Christmas morning, and yet feeling like she could never look up and face William again.

"Well," William laughed, breaking the awkwardness of the moment, "In the first place, Gary might object to that. In the second place, one has to love someone before you marry them...and I don't think Liberty really likes me that much." He proceeded to unwrap his gift with a little more speed.

"She would if you kissed her like that all the time," Heidi insisted, not wanting her super hero to disappear out of her life.

Liberty buried a very flushed face deep into her hands while Felicity used her fingers to signal to Heidi to zip her mouth shut.

William smiled at the child's innocence, somewhat enjoying Liberty's embarrassment. "Well, I'll have to keep that in mind." Then he turned to Felicity. "You have a very charming daughter."

"Yes, very charming...and very scheming." Felicity was now well aware that Heidi had set up the whole mistletoe incident, and she gave Heidi a scolding glance.

"Good qualities for an agent," William said in defense of the little girl who was now looking at them with big sad eyes, thinking that she had just ruined Christmas.

Instantly, Heidi's eyes shone and she was in heaven the rest of the morning, feeling a kindred spirit to William Casson.

Felicity finally managed to speak to William alone in the kitchen. "I'm sorry. Heidi has had it hard; first losing her father, then leaving friends and school in BC, and now me leaving for law studies. She desperately wants to hold onto everyone and keep them close...including you. I'm sorry if she caused you and Liberty any embarrassment."

William shook his head. "On the contrary. She made me feel very welcome...and...she reminds me of another little girl I used to know long ago...she also made me feel wanted...I usually don't get much of that." He smiled a quiet charming smile and opened the refrigerator to take out a bottle of ginger ale.

Felicity understood what he meant, for whatever his job entailed, she realized it was not one that attracted a welcome mat. She smiled back and returned to the living room where Heidi was chasing Liberty around the sofa with a pair of fluffy, green alligator slippers.

William could hear their laughter, and leaned against the kitchen counter with a glass of ginger ale in his hand, letting the ice cubes cool the drink before taking a sip. He didn't have to see the family fun. He closed his eyes and simply soaked in their laughter, which sounded like joyful seagulls on a beach. He took a sip from his glass and thought this was likely as close to heaven as he would get.

Gary Feddin arrived for Christmas dinner, nodding a cool greeting to William. "You're back. For how long this time?" There was a hint of sarcasm in his inquiry, for Dr. Feddin felt William endangered the Enns family, and he was not happy to see him return.

William could comprehend that the rest of the family also awaited his answer. "It depends," he said, not committing himself.

"On what?" Gary insisted, enjoying William's uneasiness, for he knew William liked to be vague about his doings, and he enjoyed forcing the man to tell more than he wanted to.

William sighed slightly in exasperation, irritated at Gary's persistent prying. "On how long it takes me to...settle some business."

"And what would that be?" Gary continued to make William squirm. Gary wanted the Enns family to realize how dangerous it was to keep William around, especially with young Heidi in the house. Of course, Gary also had an alternative motif. He was not blind to the way Liberty so readily defended the man.

William poured himself a cup of coffee. He fought quickly for an answer. "I'm looking into selling my valley farm. Anyhow, I don't like talking business on a holiday."

Gary laughed and just shook his head. He asked Liberty to take a walk with him and Heidi bit her lip because she knew what the doctor intended to ask Liberty. She could see by Liberty's nervous face that her aunt also knew Gary was planning to present her with an engagement ring. There was nothing more Heidi could do. She hoped Liberty would remember William's kiss under the mistletoe and not accept Gary's ring.

When Liberty and Gary returned from their walk, Gary entered the house with a triumphant grin on his face. Liberty's face was not so radiant, but she managed a shy smile as Gary took hold of her wrist and held her hand out so everyone could see the diamond engagement ring on her finger.

Liberty's parents hugged their daughter and new son-in-law to be, offering them congratulations, but Heidi sat beside William and didn't get off her chair. Felicity finally moved forward to embrace them, but there were mixed feelings in her heart, for she felt there was something missing in Liberty and Gary's passive relationship, and she had seen the sparks between her sister and William under the mistletoe.

William remained in shock for a few moments. Heidi saw his hands clench tightly into two fists beneath the table. Then he rose and offered his hand out to congratulate Gary. He did not embrace Liberty, but simply smiled quietly at her. As soon as the others went into the living room, he slipped on his jacket and went to exit outside.

Heidi ran to his side, "Can I go with you?"

"No! I need a few minutes alone right now...I'll be back. Don't eat all the chocolate covered nuts." He gave one of her braids an affectionate tug. "How about if I bring you back a kitten from the loft. Liberty said at suppertime that you wanted one. A kitten would cheer us up. Right?" Heidi clearly saw William's eyes mist over before he turned away.

She watched him walk slowly towards the barn, his hands shoved deep into his pockets. Cleo trailed behind, head down, almost as if he too, sensed a sadness and loss. Heidi ran into the living room and grabbed Liberty's arm. She pulled her aunt into the kitchen, explaining to the others that she had to tell Liberty a secret. "William's very sad, Aunt Liberty," she whispered so the others would not hear. "I saw tears in his eyes. You have to go talk to him or he's going to leave. I can tell. He went to the barn. Make him not leave, Aunt Liberty. Make him stay."

Liberty closed her eyes and pressed a hand over her own heart. The last thing she wanted to do was hurt William. She had hoped he would understand her engagement to Gary.

Liberty opened the barn doors slowly and saw William sitting on a pile of hay bales, head down in dismay. He straightened his posture at the sight of her, not wanting her to comprehend his disappointment at her engagement to Gary. Because he was sitting, their eyes met abreast of each other as Liberty rested both hands upon his shoulders.

"You have to understand. I don't know who you are, William...and I likely never will. But I do know the person who has given me this ring. It comes from a very good man; a friend that I know is kind and considerate, hardworking, religious, generous and faithful to me. I don't know you. I don't know what makes you happy, what makes you sad or even what ticks you off. I don't know what you dream of or what you want to do with the rest of your life. You disappear for months at a time and I don't know if you're alive or dead. I do know you are a good person inside, but that's not enough." She leaned forward and lightly kissed his cheek. "I need more in my life; something stable and...lasting...for the sake of my children someday. Take care, chameleon." She turned and ran across the barn and out the barn entrance.

William sat a long while, staring at the door. He knew he had nothing to offer her. "You can marry him," he whispered into the empty walls of the barn, "...but you will always be my lass."

After a time, he rose to his feet and glanced towards the ladder to the loft. He had promised Heidi a kitten. He climbed the ladder into the loft, and glanced about for sign of a kitten for her. He spied a fluffy orange animal in a nest of straw piled up in the far corner of the loft. The nest of straw was directly above Sundog's box stall. William approached and reached down to pick up the kitten when the floor gave way beneath his feet and he fell through the loft; man, boards, straw and kitten all landing on top of a traumatized stallion below, who proceeded to kick and trample everything and everyone in sight.

The floor fell away from beneath William's feet as if the earth had opened up and snatched him into hell. In shock, William had no time to prepare for the hurricane beneath his feet. He felt tremendous pain in his shoulder as the stallion kicked him against the box stall wall with the force of a cannon. He slid to the ground and tried to get to his feet, reaching a free arm out to quiet the terror-stricken stallion, but the animal had been frightened dramatically by the sudden avalanche falling upon him. William attempted to speak in low soothing tones to calm the horse, but nothing could undo the animal's instinct for survival. The stallion's hooves trampled and kicked at everything in his path. William tried to open the box stall door to escape the fury of Sundog's hooves, but they connected with his back and side of the head, and he dropped dazed to the ground. He felt blow after blow connect with his body until he could only lay defeated on the ground. He attempted to cover his head with a piece of broken board from the ceiling, and noted the kitten crouched beside it. With a feeble hand, he pulled the kitten close to his side so the blows from the stallion could not connect with the helpless kitten. He felt fire and ice at the same time as pain overwhelmed him and he passed into unconsciousness.

When Liberty returned from the barn, Heidi could see she had been crying. Liberty went straight to the bathroom and had not come out. Heidi waited awhile and then opened the door to see if William was also returning from the barn with her kitten. She could hear Cleo barking loudly in the barn, the stallion whinnying, and the strange sound of banging on the barn walls. "Come quick, Grampa," she screamed. "Something's wrong in the barn."

Liberty flew out of the bathroom in a flash and joined the rest as they ran towards the barn. They could hear the stallion's hooves striking the walls as they entered the barn. "Something has frightened him badly," Mike yelled as he reached the box stall door before the others. "I wish I'd grabbed the rifle." He looked inside the open door top and turned quickly to signal everyone to stay back. "Take Heidi to the house," he ordered Felicity, and Felicity's face went white, knowing something horrible had happened. "Donna, go around and open the outside door and let Sundog into the corral." Donna obeyed without question and ran quickly to open the box stall door to the outdoors.

Liberty brushed past her father and looked into the box stall. "Oh God, no!" The breath escaped from her like a broken balloon and her knees slightly buckled. Gary grabbed to steady her and then peered into the box stall. He instantly whipped out his cell to call for the ambulance. As soon as Donna had the stallion out of the stall, Gary charged in to help William.

Liberty kneeled beside William's trampled body, and gently brushed the straw off his face and out of his brown hair. "Please don't be dead, William. Please don't be."

Gary searched for a pulse and gave her a small reassurance. "I've got a pulse, but goodness knows how broken he is inside. Sundog really pounded him into the ground."

William's eyes opened faintly and a relieved Liberty bent close to smile at him. William uttered weakly, "I must be in hell."

Liberty's eyebrows arched in surprise because she did not expect his first reaction to be so negative upon seeing her face.

"...because I feel like shit," he added with a faint, teasing smile that was half grimace of pain. Then he faded into unconsciousness again.

"He still has his wits about him, so that's a good sign, isn't it?" Mike asked the doctor, looking for some reassurance for Liberty's sake.

Donna grabbed a horse blanket and covered William carefully.

"Anything is better than nothing, but I'm not going to lie. He's been trampled badly. Might have internal bleeding. Be careful with him."

William moaned and moved his legs about in pain. "Good sign that he can move his legs though," Gary informed them, knowing the family needed some sign of hope.

Suddenly, an orange kitten head popped up beside William, and Liberty grabbed the little ball of fluff. "Oh, Gary!" Liberty whispered, her voice full of tenderness. "He was getting Heidi a kitten from the loft."

Mike looked up at the hole in the ceiling, and picked up a broken board strewn in the straw. "That floor was solid as rock. The boards have obviously been cut, and then replaced. Someone set a trap for him and I think we know who. But how on earth would he know that William would be entering the loft to get a kitten? When would he cut the boards and prepare all of this?"

William began mumbling in a foreign language that none of them could interpret.

"I think it's Italian," Gary decided. "Contelli, the barber is always yelling and throwing things at Mrs. Beechwood's cat. I think some of the words sound familiar."

"He's probably used to speaking Italian," Mike added without realizing he was revealing information Gary knew nothing about. "Joel said Tony McTavish was actually Anthony Antonio from the Italian mafia many years ago."

Gary stared at Donna and Mike in horror, "Are you kidding? You knew that and yet you let this man stay in your house? My God! It could have been Heidi in the loft looking for a kitten. Why would you harbor someone from the mafia?" Gary could not understand.

William moaned again and mumbled in Italian, "Lisciare li solo! Essi sapere niente (*Leave them alone! They know nothing!*)!"

"Tony's involvement with the mafia was long before he took William in as a child," Mike informed Gary. "Tony was reported dead before he went to Ireland and took up with William. I don't think William has any tie with the mafia. None of their doings seem to play into what William and Tony were about."

Gary mumbled partly under his breath, "Then I hate to think what he's mixed up in if it's worse than the mafia."

Suddenly, Gary thought of Felicity. "Say, one of you better go tell Felicity what's going on. She'll be worried half to death." Then he turned to Liberty. "I'm taking William straight to Regina in the ambulance. If he needs any kind of surgery, he's better there than our small hospital. If you want to stay with him, better rush and pack an overnight case, because once he's in the ambulance, I'm not stopping until he's in Regina."

Liberty grabbed the kitten for Heidi, and rushed to the house to inform Felicity on what had happened to William. Liberty raced quickly upstairs to her bedroom to pack a few essentials and change of clothing. In the distance, she could hear ambulance sirens, and prayed for William's life.

Mike put a sympathetic hand on Gary's shoulder. "That

was thoughtful of you to do that for Liberty. I know it's not easy for you. Liberty has some strange tie to this guy."

"Yeah! I can see that." Gary pulled the blanket more carefully about William. "She was always one to take in strays. Well, I won't lie to you, Mike. I think he may be bust up bad inside. Let her be there to say her goodbyes to him if the worst happens. I know Liberty. She'll never heal if she's not there to convince herself there was nothing more she could do for him."

Mike nodded in agreement, knowing that Gary understood his daughter even better than he did.

The ambulance pulled into the yard with lights flashing and sirens wailing loudly. Cleo let out a mournful howl as Mike hurried to the barn door to wave them over to the barn entrance.

Once again, Liberty sat by William's hospital bed, waiting for him to regain consciousness. She realized getting injured was part of the chance he took every day in his line of work, but seeing him lying here injured again made her angry. Examinations showed he had a broken collar bone and arm, concussion and another broken rib. He was also badly bruised from numerous blows by Sundog's hooves, but luckily no internal bleeding was so far detected. William's midriff had been somewhat protected by the extra padding of his winter coat.

The door opened gingerly, and Jo Wong slipped into the hospital room, his eyes darting to and fro to make sure no one else but Liberty was in the room. "I know it says no visitors," Jo whispered quickly to Liberty, giving her no time to dismiss him from the room, "but I had to see how he was. We'll get Fox. I promise."

Liberty stared at Jo Wong. "I should have guessed that you were an agent too when I saw you talking together." She looked back down at William bitterly. "We don't know if he'll regain consciousness or not. He had a bad concussion only a few months ago and now another. Look!" she said angrily, staring down at William's bruised and bandaged body. "Look what Fox did to him. Look what POLLU has done to him...made him a sacrificial lamb just to catch Fox. You tell your boss he's finished with this stupidity. He's..."

Jo Wong put his hand over her mouth to silence her. "Sssh! You do not know who he is. Don't belittle what he does." He withdrew his hand gently from her lips, and sympathetically rested a hand on her shoulder. He stared into her eyes with meaningful contact. "Don't you ever forget who he is. He's a chameleon. POLLU can never replace him." Jo Wong turned and exited the room. Then he put his head back inside the door. "Oh, and agents are stationed outside this door for the length of his stay. You won't know who they are, but they're there. Feel safe." Then he was gone.

Liberty felt weak and more alone than she had ever been in her life. She knew secrets about William's life that she could not discuss with the rest of the world. She twirled the engagement ring on her finger, watching the diamond twinkle in the light. The ring offered her a good secure life with a dear friend that she could trust, but the man lying beside her consumed her thoughts, and she didn't know how to let him go. The choice between William and Gary was easy to calculate. Gary would make her first in his life and William would make her last. It was as simple as that. She thought of Jo Wong's wife. Did she know her husband was an agent for POLLU? How did she cope when he was gone for months at a time, not there to share in their daughter's accomplishments, never knowing where he was or what he was doing or if he was still alive. She felt a strong new apathy for the wives of soldiers.

William's eyes flickered and tried to open, having difficulty to focus for a few moments. Liberty leaned over William, relieved to have him finally regain consciousness. It had been three days of unbearable waiting and she was exhausted from worry.

"It wasn't...the stallion's fault," he whispered weakly.

Liberty reassured him, "We know. He'll be alright. Now you rest."

"Fox...got to me again...didn't he?"

"I'm afraid so. He cut a hole in the loft floor so you would fall through into the stallion's box stall. Evil man, that guy! Oh, and Jo Wong was here. He said there's agents guarding outside, so rest easy. Now I'm going to notify the doctors. They'll want to know that you've regained consciousness." Liberty reached out her hand to ring the buzzer, but he intercepted and weakly slipped his fingers around hers, needing the strength that holding her hand could give him. He was about to say something, then felt the engagement ring still on her finger and released her hand as gently as he had sought it. A light faded in his eyes.

Two doctors suddenly entered the room, their white smocks floating like sheets on a clothes line. Dr. Anne Jacobson grinned a wide smile, pleased to see his improved condition. "And how is our sleepy patient feeling?"

William closed his eyes, not wanting to talk to anyone at this moment. There were lines of pain etched across his forehead. "Like I've gone to hell...and back again," he answered truthfully.

The doctor sympathized. "Well, you've been battered about quite badly, but fortunately no internal bleeding. We'll be keeping a check on that for a bit. First, I simply want to enjoy the pleasure of seeing you awake."

William wanted to escape the doctor's cheerful voice, so he kept his eyes closed. Their voices gradually became distant to him, and he couldn't distinguish what they were saying as he slipped into unconsciousness again.

Joel Fluery called a meeting in the local municipal office and now rose to address the invited persons. Mike and Donna Enns were in attendance, as well as Felicity, Dr. Feddin and a number of local farmers who lived on the circumference of the Enns farm.

"First of all," Joel began, "I know you are familiar with William Casson and that he has been staying off and on with the Enns family. You've also heard by now that another attack took place on his life on Christmas Day and that William is in the hospital at Regina. Liberty has been keeping us posted on his condition. As of now, he's drifting in and out of a comma."

Joel put both hands on the table and leaned forward with urgency. "I would like all of you to investigate your outsheds, check your property for unusual tracks, and if anything looks out of the ordinary, report anything suspicious back to me. Don't approach anyone, just report back. This maniac must have been lurking around our area somewhere."

Bill Hogkins spoke up loudly. "Then maybe Casson should stay the heck out of Glenfield and this nut wouldn't follow him in here. We got family to think about." Bill Hogkins had always been in opposition to William Casson lingering in the community.

Gil Martin cut in to soothe the matter a little. "It's not that we don't feel for the boy, Mike. He's been beaten and left to burn to death and now set up to be trampled by your stud, but you gotta admit he who lives by the sword, dies by the sword, and I have a feeling this kid has done a lot of sword fighting in his day."

Mike and Donna exchanged glances for they knew Gil Martin was right. Mike stood up to get their attention. "We understand your concerns. We're not asking you for much...just that you check around and report anything unusual to Constable Fluery. Do it for your own safety, if not for Casson."

Bill Hogkins huffed in disgust, "Yeah, well, guess we can't do much else now." Hogkins turned to Dr. Feddin for input into the conversation. Hogkins knew rumors had spread about a relationship between Liberty and William, so he hoped Dr. Feddin would have a negative opinion on Casson. "What's your take on it, Doc?"

Dr. Feddin looked a bit awkward. As doctor of the community, he felt he should keep a neutral opinion on just about everything from politics to who baked the best pie at the local fair. He guarded every word spoken. "I feel whoever William works for must be watching over him."

"Well, they're doing a damn poor job of it, I'd say," chirped in old Shuster, pulling his elastic suspenders out a few inches and then letting them snap back against his chest.

Hogkins growled at Shuster, hoping the elderly man had not slowed Dr. Feddin's momentum. "Let the Doc say his peace."

Shuster shrunk back in his chair and decided he had done his duty just by opening his mouth.

"It won't hurt to keep our eyes open," the doctor continued. "But like I said before, I feel whoever William works for hasn't just walked away from him, so they'll be around here too... somewhere...whoever they are."

"I say we take a vote on whether we let him back in this community or not," Hogkins suggested, feeling he now had a slight edge on a decision to get rid of William.

Old Shuster gave Hogkin's shoulder a pat. "Come on now, Bill. You've been suspicious of Casson ever since last September when you left Kel's Bar, and thought you heard Casson speaking Chinese in the back alley to Jo Wong." Shuster gave a hearty laugh. "Bill thinks everyone is talking Chinese when he's had a few drinks too many." Everyone chuckled except Bill Hogkins, whose face became a blustery shade of red.

"They were up to something," Bill voiced strongly, believing with his whole heart that he had witnessed their conversation in Chinese.

Joel Fluery tilted his head to the side like a hawk that has just caught sight of movement in the grass. "Did you say you thought William was talking to Jo Wong in Chinese?"

Suddenly the door opened, and Heidi entered gingerly. She walked to the meeting table, clutching her school bag tight enough to bare her knuckles white. She had been waiting in the corridor, trying to gather enough courage to enter the meeting.

"We'll be done in a few moments, dear," Felicity informed her gently.

Heidi looked up with two huge uneasy eyes. "I think I know how the bad man found out William was going to get me a kitten in the loft." Silence fell across the meeting table as Heidi slowly pulled her diary out of her school bag and laid the book on the table. "He read my diary," she said, and a murmur of astonishment circled the room.

Felicity put her hand to her mouth and gasped in horror

to think William's attacker had been watching her young daughter close enough to see her write in her diary.

Dr. Feddin calmly put his arm around the uneasy child. "Show us where, honey," Gary said softly, and pulled the book in front of her, so that she could open it.

"But you'll be mad at me if you read it," she said to Dr. Feddin, her eyes misting over with tears.

"Me? Why would I be mad?"

"Because I wrote in the diary that I wanted Aunt Liberty to marry William, not you."

Mike Enns ran fingers through his sparse threads of grey hair, while his wife put a hand to her forehead and awkwardly looked down at the table. Felicity's mouth opened in shock and then saddened to think Heidi had caused Gary public embarrassment. The neighbors simply shifted uncomfortably in their chairs around the meeting table and never said a word.

"That's okay, honey," Dr. Feddin sighed. "If I had to choose between myself and a hero who could fly around with a red cape on, I'd chose him too. Now you show us where you wrote about the kitten." He wrapped his arms around Heidi and she snuggled safely against his chest. She opened the diary and turned to the page about the kitten in the loft.

Felicity watched the two of them together, and warmth crept across her skin. All her life, she had sought adventure and teased the quiet, studious Gary Feddin. She had taken his quietness as timidness, but now she could see that was not so. As she watched him handle her child and the situation with great class and humility, she wondered what other qualities she had overlooked in Dr. Feddin.

Then Felicity jolted back to the reality that William's attacker had somehow acquired her daughter's diary. "How would he know about the diary?" Her heartbeat quickened at the thought of Heidi being watched.

"I think he saw me writing in it through my window. I heard something outside the window one night, but I didn't want to call everyone again, because I lied when..." Sobs interrupted Heidi's explanation.

"Cleo...the dog...followed his trail down to the river the next morning...almost to your hunting cabin, Gil," Mike interrupted, exploding with fresh knowledge. "I think he's at Martin's cabin!"

"Okay! "Joel said with equal excitement. "All of you return home and say nothing to anyone. I'm calling for backup from the Milford detachment. I think something constructive might have come out of this."
"I've got a couple snowmobiles that you can use," Hogkins offered willingly, and they left the meeting room in a hurry.

"I better get back to the hospital," Gary said shyly to Felicity. "Maybe Liberty has called." He reached out and playfully flipped Heidi's scarf over her eyes. "I'll let you know how Super Wil is doing. Okay?" Then he turned and walked towards his car.

"I guess he's okay for Aunt Liberty," Heidi informed her mother, as she took her mother's hand and walked towards the parking lot.
"He's okay for anybody," Felicity replied softly, her cheeks flushing slightly in the crisp January air. She was ashamed that she should be forming any such opinion on her sister's fiancé'.

Suddenly Dr. Feddin turned on his heel and returned to where Felicity and her daughter were getting in their car. "Heidi," he asked curiously, "Why would you rather have Liberty marry William?"

"Because she hums songs when she thinks he's coming home," Heidi replied with a child's simple honesty.

He nodded his head in acknowledgement and walked back to his own vehicle. It was a good answer.

It was shortly after two o'clock in the morning when William opened his eyes and focused in on Strauz sitting like a buzzard at his bedside. "Now I know I've died and gone to hell," William said painfully, as he attempted to move his sore body to a different position.

"Glad to see you're back to normal," Strauz answered, trying to erase any sign of concern off his face. "Can't talk long before the nurses discover I'm here, but I have a proposition for you, William."

William never liked it when he was addressed so informally. Whenever Strauz got personal, he was scheming something.

"You've had two bad concussions within several months. The next time, I'm afraid you may not wake up. You're too valuable for POLLU to lose that way." Captain Strauz rose to his feet as if he had little time left for discussion. "I'm going to be stepping down as Captain for about six months...a little surgery that needs attending to...and I need a temporary replacement. You've been with us since you were eight years old and I figure you could offer POLLU a lot as Assistant Captain. Get you out of the field and into a safer environment for that brilliant mind of yours for about six months. Let you heal a bit."

"I thought you were planning to have me pose as a priest to gain Sinclair Molley's confidence," William replied with a bit of apprehension in his voice. "I've been practicing patience."

The Captain scoffed with amusement, knowing William would have to practice patience a long time to gain any of it. "That mission is pending. Kind of hard for you to appear like a priest when you look like you've been boxing with a kangaroo. I want you out of action for a while. It'll be good for you to be Assistant Captain for a few months. Maybe you'll learn to appreciate what I do for a change."

"You know how I feel about some of POLLU's policies," William refreshed Strauz's memory. "You might not recognize the Agency when you get back."

Strauz narrowed his eyes into two catlike slits. "I think you know just how far I can be pushed, chameleon, so don't step too far over the line."

William studied his Captain deeply. It was not like Strauz to even slightly consider giving him chance to tamper with his policies. Over the years, the two of them had been in many conflicts over their differences; one working for the good of the whole, and one working for the good of the individual. "You know my value to you is not in a leadership role," William informed him. "I have a tendency to travel my own path. You know I best serve POLLU as a chameleon."

"Not if you're brain dead," the Captain snapped back, looking at his watch impatiently again, and checking the door for sign of anyone approaching.

"How many times have you called me a wildcard?" William persisted, still struggling to raise himself into a sitting position. "I'm the last person you would consider for Assistant Captain. What's up?"

114

"Take it as a moment of weakness on my part, but I am going to give you a chance to either serve POLLU or leave. You can't have it both ways. You can be anything from a diplomat to a prince. Name it and I can personally see that you are placed in that position, if you don't want to stay with POLLU."

"You mean do one thing for the rest of my life?" William inquired apprehensively. The thought made him nervous.

"Isn't that what you've always wanted?"

"I suppose...but...once you've trained a dog to chase foxes, it's kind of hard to make him stop." William felt like he was suddenly thrown in a closet with no air.

"So then what do you want? I'm letting you go. Can't you see that?...Name it. What do you want to be? You're either in POLLU or you're out. No half way anymore. The offer is only good until the first nurse comes through that door. Then I'm gone."

William looked at the sterile white walls of the hospital. He was free. He had finally escaped POLLU. But for the first time in his life, he was afraid of being something other than what he was...and he was good at what he was. He could chose to be one person, but what would he do with the other thousands of people he was now trained to be? They were part of him too; their occupations, their cultures and languages, their knowledge. Would he soon feel unfulfilled if he never used these skills again? He glanced nervously about the room, as if looking for an escape from the decision. Liberty would be marrying the doctor. He had no other dreams without her. He inhaled deeply and the words came out of his mouth without him realizing it. "Then I chose to be a chameleon."

"Granted", Strauz said and turned like a soldier on his heels and left before William could change his mind. As Strauz walked down the hospital corridor, a satisfying smile crossed his face. Strauz was a sly man at strategy. "Happy New Year!", he expressed joyfully into the empty chamber of an elevator that carried him down and out of the hospital. If it had not been that Strauz was in a public place, the normally stern man would have jumped in the air and clicked his heels like a clown. Keeping William Casson in the POLLU agency was like winning the Lotto.

Liberty juggled an armful of magazines and a coffee cup as she entered William's hospital room. Her face beamed with relief upon seeing him sitting partly upright and conscious. "Well, I'm glad to see you're awake again." She dumped the magazines on a chair and sat the coffee cup on a window sill.

"What day is it?" William asked, wincing in pain as he moved positions in the bed.

Liberty helped him sit more upright and fluffed up the pillows behind his head and shoulders. "You've been in and out of a comma for over a week, but this is the brightest that I've seen you, so that's a relief."
"I'm hungry."

She smiled. "Good sign! I'll go see what they'll allow you to have. The doctor will want to know you're awake...Oh, and we discovered how Fox knew you would be looking for a kitten in the loft. He read Heidi's diary. She mentioned that you were going to get her one from the loft... Also, Dad said they figured Fox had been staying at Martin's hunting cabin near our place, so Constable Fluery and the Milford detachment are checking that out." Then Liberty's voice trailed in despair, "What twisted mind would think to cut a hole in a loft floor above a stallion?"

"One would have to get inside his head to figure that out,"

William sighed. Suddenly, an idea enlightened his thoughts and his eyes began to sparkle. "Okay, say we're him. He's done his deed for this time. He'll go off to celebrate, feel good for a while until the next time. He wasn't one to enjoy anything but his work, but his lab is now destroyed by POLLU, so he can't go there. I worked with him for eight months in the laboratory, so I know his habits. Relaxing on a beach just wasn't his way to celebrate." William's heart quickened like a bloodhound that catches the first scent of a trail. He attempted to swing his legs over the side of the bed, but Liberty intervened.

"Hey, take it easy! The doctors need to examine you before you try anything like that." She tucked the blankets in tight around him to prevent him from trying to get out of the bed again. William protested but her precautionary nursing instincts won the argument.

"You stay put until they say it's okay. So where do you think Fox might go if he were to celebrate?" Liberty asked eagerly, guarding his bedside so he would stay stationary until his condition was checked by doctors.

William leaned his head back deeply into his pillow and went silent in thought, his mind tracing Dwight Fox's footsteps as if he was the man himself. Finally he spoke his thoughts aloud. "He'll want to go somewhere to celebrate his revenge, somewhere personal, some..." William's voice trailed off and he looked Liberty square in the eye. "Somewhere like where his children are buried, so he can celebrate with them."

Liberty touched his hand, a chill running through her veins that frightened and thrilled her at the same time. "Would he still be there?"   "Where else? Their graves are the only thing he has left to return to and to share his victory with."

"I almost feel sorry for him," Liberty expressed sadly.

"Aye! Too bad his kids got caught in the middle." William inched himself closer to the edge of the bed, hoping she wouldn't notice.

"Where are his children buried?"

"His ex-wife lives in Spain, so the children are buried there."

Liberty deliberated for a few moments. "Would he return to his wife?"

"No! She would have him shot. She blames the death of her children on his connection with terrorists...and rightfully so." William looked around the room. "Are my clothes in the closet?"

Liberty put her hands firmly on her hips. "You won't be in any shape for traveling for a while. Forget your clothes. Can't you get POLLU to trap him there?"

"Can't chance it. If I lose this opportunity to catch him, I may never get another before he drops me into a volcano or something. I'm going to have to go myself."

"No! You can't. You are not well enough to travel, especially in an airplane with a fresh concussion. Besides, do you honestly think you can handle Fox in your condition, broken bones and all?" Liberty refused to let William even consider getting out of his hospital bed.

"Then come with me...as my nurse, and get hold of Jo Wong. Tell him I need him here pronto." William's blue eyes were clearly serious and Liberty could see nothing would change his mind about going to Spain, with or without her.

"How will I explain this to my folks and Gary? I just can't up and go with you. I don't even know if my passport is up to date. Do I need shots? Do I go home for clothes?"

"No. You go straight to Jo Wong. Don't contact your family or Gary. It's too risky. Only speak to Jo Wong in person and do as he says. Don't worry about passports or other stuff. Wong will arrange all that. Now go!"

Liberty touched his arm. "I'm afraid for your health, William...and my folks and Gary are going to worry half to death if I just up and disappear. Please don't make me do this."

William ignored her plea and swung his legs over the bedside. "Jo Wong will sort everything out. Now go! Don't waste any time. Ring the bell for the doctors. I'm sure they'll examine me before you get back, and then we'll know what condition I'm in. How's that?...But I'm leaving regardless of what they say. You realize that."

Liberty simply shook her head at him in disgust, and stomped out of the hospital room.

As Liberty drove down the highway, her mind raced in a million directions. "What in the world have I got myself into?" she asked herself. "What am I doing engaged to Gary and flying off to Spain with William to find a madman. I've completely lost my mind."

Joel Fluery hadn't slept a minute all night, disappointed that the local police detachments had been unsuccessful in finding William's attacker at Martin's hunting cabin. Perhaps the finger printing and collecting DNA samples taken from the cabin might reveal who the attacker was, but for now, he was at a dead end again. He remembered Shuster kidding Bill about hearing William speak in Chinese to Jo Wong. According to others, William had also spoken Italian from time to time, even German. There had to be some connection with William's ability to speak foreign languages. He swung his legs out of bed and decided to take an innocent-looking, morning walk with his dog. He did not want any town gossip to form from sighting his police car in the Wong driveway.

Joel knocked on the front door of Jo Wong's house. A smiling twelve year old greeted him heartily. "Poppa says for you to come in for coffee. He saw you coming up the walk."

Joel tied his dog to the stair railing, and entered the house. "Hi, Cherie!" he smiled and held her two black ponytails out like airplane wings. "Are you flying to school this morning?"

She giggled and ran upstairs in her nightgown. Jo Wong's wife smiled at him from the kitchen doorway. "Bring your dog in out of the cold. Fresh muffins and coffee are on the table. I'll leave you alone with Jo." She followed her daughter upstairs.

Joel stepped back out onto the porch and untied his dog. He reentered and instructed his black, Labrador dog to stay on the doormat. Jo Wong gestured for Joel to sit down, and poured him a cup of coffee. "I imagine you're here about William," Jo said, coming right to the matter at hand.

"You know him well?" Joel decided to start his questioning slow. He reached for a raspberry muffin, a favorite of Joel's every time he went to their restaurant.

"I don't think anyone really knows William," Jo commented honestly, knowing that William kept a lot of his thoughts to himself.
"You arrived here about two years ago, and William and Tony slightly over one. Is there any coincidence to that?"

Jo Wong spread butter on a muffin slowly, contemplating how to word his next reply. "What are you wanting to know, Constable? No sense dancing around the table."

"I want to know what your connection is with William. I want to know why he's here in Glenfield, and who the hell is trying to kill him and why. I have a feeling you know the answers."

"You're not asking for much, are you?...First, our connection is business related. Secondly, he came here to set a trap for a troubled individual who is trying to eventually kill him. Lastly, the attacker blames William for an incident that took some of his family members. It's a case of revenge. Now I must get to the restaurant."

Constable Fluery was about to leave the kitchen when the front door flew open, and Liberty stumbled over his dog sprawled on the doormat. A distraught Liberty yelled out, "Jo, you have to help William quick. He has to fly to Spain immediately to catch Fox. We think he's..." Liberty suddenly noticed Constable Fluery standing beside the kitchen table, and her tongue froze solid.

Liberty looked at Jo Wong for direction on what to do next, and Jo took a deep breath. "I guess you're now involved, Constable, whether you wish to be or not. Sit down and I'll fill you in. Liberty, come tell us what's up. We can trust Joel."

After fifteen minutes of hasty explanation, they made plans to pick William up from the hospital and arrange flights to Spain for the threesome of William, Liberty and Wong. Although Jo Wong knew Strauz had stationed other agents in the area, he felt more confident trusting solely in Joel's loyalty. They agreed to keep their plans within their small circle for fear word may leak back to Fox.

Liberty was nauseous to think of how her family and Gary would worry at her disappearance, so Wong instructed Joel to tell them that due to security, William and Liberty were placed in a protection plan until Fox was caught. It would perhaps ease their worry about her safety from Fox. It would not, however, ease Gary's worry about her safety from William.
Liberty soon discovered that Jo Wong had connections that would astound any worldly network. Guarding a chameleon made services available to him that few others could

obtain. Governments opened doors for the POLLU agency.

Jo accompanied Liberty back to Regina to pick up William. Along the way, he stopped and made a number of phone calls, speaking in several foreign languages.

"You and William are quite fluent in languages," Liberty said to him, thinking of how many times she had seen him cooking in his humble restaurant, and never imagined him as working for a secret agency.

"Necessary for the job," he smiled, "although I'm not as trained in languages as William. I think he can speak eleven...fluently. And another dozen moderately. It allows him to work anywhere in the world."
"That's amazing."

"Yes. He's rather amazing at everything...except guarding himself." He laughed good naturedly." I excel at being a watchdog better than him. He sucks at that."

"It's good to know he's not perfect," Liberty laughed, and Jo Wong grinned back, knowing they both understood William wasn't far off of perfection at doing everything else.

Slipping William out of the hospital undetected took some planning. Necessary forms needed to be signed in order to be released against a doctor's advice. Such permission to leave would create delays that Wong did not feel they had time for, so they slipped secretly out of the hospital and into an ambulance.

Wong arranged for a private plane at a smaller airport. It was not an easy task to file and have a flight plan accepted in such a tight time frame. Arranging the flight as a health emergency for a patient to receive a heart transplant in Toronto was only done through permission from higher authorities. Jo Wong was a master at such planning, and his connections gave him the ability to carry them out successfully.

"Drive to the Sandhills Airport, a small airport outside of Regina," he instructed Liberty. "Here's the directions. Meet us there. Buy William new clothing. He will be in hospital attire when I arrive. Pick up any medical supplies that you think William might need...and anything you may need yourself." He handed her a fistful of money. "Do it quickly! We'll stop in a small airport outside Toronto, then take a regular flight to Spain. I've already booked our tickets." Jo Wong slipped out of the car and disappeared into the crowded street, not wasting any more time explaining.

Liberty waited anxiously in her car at the Sandhills Airport. She could see a small plane waiting on the runway, and figured it must be their flight, as no other planes looked ready for takeoff. Suddenly an ambulance drove onto the runway and approached the airplane. She recognized Jo Wong step out of the ambulance, dressed in a white doctor smock. He began wheeling William on a stretcher towards the plane. She joined the procession without saying a word, and watched as several attendants helped Wong load William onto the plane.

A tall man of African descent looked both ways to see that no one was listening and then spoke to Wong in secretive tones. Wong nodded his head and slapped the man on the shoulder as if in agreement. Wong returned to Liberty and gestured for her to get into the plane quickly. "He's worried you're not an agent. I told him you were William's nurse."

"So did that satisfy him?"

Wong hurried her up the steps into the plane. "He said that was okay. We can dispose of you later."

Liberty swallowed. She was never too sure if Wong was joking or not.

Once in the plane with the doors closed, Jo freed William from being strapped to the stretcher, and William slipped into the pilot's seat. His forehead wrinkled with a measure of pain every time he moved his injured body. Wong seated himself as co-pilot and Liberty's mouth dropped open in shock. Not a word escaped her lips as they whisked down the runway and lifted off into the sky.

Then her patience burst. "I don't believe this! I'm flying in a plane with a one-armed pilot in his hospital pajamas, and a sushi cook in a doctor's smock for a co-pilot."

Both the men exploded in laughter. William glanced back and grinned at her. "You've never been safer."

Liberty huffed in opposition to that statement. "Forgive me if I don't believe you."

Liberty heard William give a slight moan now and then when the plane rocked in turbulence, and she knew he must be suffering far more than he was trying to reveal.

Hours later, they notified her that they were nearing the small airport outside of Toronto. William asked for the clothing that she had bought for him, removed the sling supporting his arm and shoulder, and changed into the clothing. Then he returned to the cockpit. They brought the plane down somewhat roughly, but at least it came to a stop.

"I'm better at flying jets," William excused his rough landing with a grin, and for some strange reason, she almost believed him.

Liberty followed the two men to where a cab was waiting to take them to the Toronto Airport. Wong handed passports and tickets to William and Liberty and all three waited apprehensively in the lineup to board the Toronto-based plane on route to Spain. Liberty was terrified that they would be intercepted and hauled off by the authorities. She did not want to even ask how or where Wong got passports. Perhaps their duplicates had been quickly granted. She didn't want to know.

All went well for them passing through customs. The men carried little luggage and were seasoned travelers. Once in Spain, they spoke Spanish as if they had been born Spaniards. Liberty just followed along, for she knew nothing of what they planned and had to trust in their judgment.

Their cab dropped them off at a small motel where Wong had made previous arrangements for a room. Liberty flung herself across one of the two beds, exhausted from the events. William practically collapsed into a chair and lowered his head to his knees as he clutched his broken arm and shoulder with one free arm. They had left his broken collarbone and arm without support for fear of William being easily spotted in public with an injury. He had not complained and only now did the pain of his injuries truly surface. Liberty immediately came to his side, opening her bag to bring out medical supplies. "Take these pain killers," she offered with a glass of water. "I'll make another sling to support your arm and shoulder. And let me check the bandages on your ribs."

William obeyed without saying anything. His eyes were dull and tired and she knew his energy was completely spent.

"Time for you to rest, chameleon," Wong ordered. "First bed is yours. I'm going out to check a few things, get us a few weapons, check if anyone's around the cemetery. I'll bring back some food." He opened his brief case and pressed a beard onto his chin for disguise. "Stay inside and lock the door."

William wandered over to a bed and dropped down upon it. In minutes, he was asleep. Liberty removed his shoes and lay a blanket across him. She sat on the bed beside him and watched him sleep for a while to make sure he was alright. Besides his more serious injuries, she knew he was badly bruised from being kicked and trampled by the stallion. The flights had also been extremely hard on him.

She looked down at the engagement ring on her finger and wondered if Gary was frantic with worry over her. He would be furious at William for getting her into this mess. Then exhausted herself, she lay down beside William, feeling safer if she lay close to his side. She soon drifted off to sleep.

Wong unlocked the door and entered quietly. Seeing the two asleep side by side, he placed the food in a small refrigerator, and spread a blanket over Liberty. Then he took the other bed, glad to have the extra space for himself.

Wong explained the next morning that there was evidence someone had returned to the graves, for he could see fresh flowers lain, but he had kept his distance in case Fox was watching. He slapped a couple pistols and knives on the table and Liberty shivered distastefully to think they would consider using them. He tossed a shawl for her to wear over her head, and both he and William proceeded to disguise their faces. William wrapped a cape about his shoulders to hide the fact that his one arm was in a sling.

The motel was tucked in a hillside and they dismounted several layers of steps before coming out onto a more level street below. Liberty could see the ocean waters lapping at the cliff face and wished her visit to beautiful Spain had been under different circumstances.

William hailed down an old truck passing by, spoke in Spanish to the driver and handed him some pesos. Then he gestured for the others to jump in the back of the truck. He sat beside Liberty in a pile of straw and explained to her with an elfish grin. "Untraceable taxi service!" Liberty had a feeling William was slightly enjoying keeping her in suspense.

The truck dropped them off near the cemetery. Wong separated from the two, so as not to cause suspicion, and circled the far side of the cemetery. William bent down, swiped a bouquet of flowers from a grave near his feet, and placed them in Liberty's arms. An old woman walking by shook her head at them in disgust, and Liberty wanted to die of humiliation.

"What an awful thing to do," she scolded William in a hushed tone.

"Trust me! I've done worse... Now pretend we are a grieving couple, pull your shawl up over your face, and we'll pay our respects to the grave beside Fox's children."

Liberty obeyed and they walked slowly towards the site. There was no sign of Fox, but that did not mean he wasn't watching from somewhere.

Liberty elbowed William. "Aah, look! His daughter was near the same age as Heidi... And there's a note pinned to the flowers. I don't know if I can read it." She squinted her eyes to read the note without looking obvious to anyone who might be watching. "It says, " *An eye for an eye...and a child for a chi...*"

William grabbed her arm and started running across the cemetery towards Wong. The flowers flew from her arms, leaving a rainbow trail of petals across the cemetery. "He left a note for me. He's after Heidi," William yelled frantically to Wong, and Jo whipped out his cell phone and started dialing the Enns household.

A terrified voice answered the Enns phone. "He's got her," Donna Enns sobbed to Jo Wong. "He took her right off the school bus and told the driver he'd shoot the whole bus of kids if he tried to stop him. He's got her. He told the bus driver he wants William to watch her die just like he saw his daughter and son die. Oh dear God, we should never have brought Heidi here."

Liberty grabbed the phone from Wong's hand. "Mom! Mom! Please don't cry. Where's Felicity?"

"She's here, but she's absolutely devastated, and I don't think she's even capable of talking right now. Where are you, Liberty? Are you okay?"

Liberty's hands were shaking so badly that William gently took the phone out of her hands. "I'm sorry, Mrs. Enns. More sorry than you'll ever know. Fox won't do anything until I return. We'll get him first. Trust me!...and Liberty is okay. She's with me."

Donna didn't answer. Being with William wasn't exactly the safest place to be. Donna slowly hung up the phone, and the weight of the world fell on William's shoulders.

"I think we need Strauz this time," Wong suggested, and William nodded in agreement.

Jo Wong and Liberty returned to Glenfield, but William did not. He flew straight to Germany to plan a strategy with the cunning Strauz. Strauz was not happy that William and Jo Wong had tried to trap Fox in Spain without his knowledge, but he wasted no time dwelling on the matter. The situation with Heidi was the present problem. There was time enough for reprimanding William and Jo Wong later.

"You realize she's just one child," Strauz said to William, "And I have thirty thousand of them just like her that I'm trying to save elsewhere at this moment. Do you expect me to pull my resources from other countries to help this one child? I already have a dozen agents watching you, and not one has caught so much as a shadow of Fox."

William sighed. "He's one step ahead of me no matter what I do."

"How smart is the child?" Strauz asked, looking out the

office window with his back to William.

"Real smart!"

Strauz turned and rested his hands on his desk. "Then trust in her."

William rose to his feet, disheartened that Strauz was unable to offer him extra manpower. As he took the elevator down and out of the building, he thought about Strauz's words. Heidi would not sit idle with her kidnapper. She had a flare for detective and spy work, and would be looking for a way to leave clues on her location. Perhaps she had left clues already.

He dared not return to Glenfield for fear it might signal Fox to kill Heidi in front of him. He would have to return in disguise. At least, Strauz could arrange that for him.

Heidi looked at the four barren walls in the large walk-in closet that Fox had tossed her into. Other than a blanket on the floor and a light bulb in the ceiling, there was nothing, not a window or a clothes hanger. She curled up in the blanket and cuddled into a corner, wondering what Fox was going to do with her. Heidi didn't want her kidnapper to hear her crying, so she buried her face deep in the blanket.

The next morning, she yelled through the door, "I have to go to the bathroom," and a cold faced man with an unshaved face yanked the door open and pointed to a room beside the closet. She walked past him haughtily and into the bathroom.

"If you try to escape through the window, I'll cut your legs off when you're half-way out," Fox yelled viciously to her, so Heidi quickly snuffed that idea from her head. She stuffed a length of toilet paper in her pocket. Then she stood on the toilet seat and looked through the window, trying to figure out where she was located. She could see factory smoke stacks, but that was about all.

Once back in the large walk-in closet, she proceeded to write carefully on every section of the tissue with a pencil that she had in her pocket. "*I'm kidnapped. Help! Room faces smoke stacks. Call Constable Fluery,Glenfield.* "Then she added her grandparent's phone number to the bottom of the notes. She counted fourteen notes. That meant fourteen chances to contact help if she ever got out of this room. She folded each separately and slipped them back into her pocket.

Around noon, her closet door opened slightly and a can of cola and a large piece of pizza slid across the floor like two curling rocks. Then the door slammed shut again. It was going to be difficult to distribute her messages unless she could get out into public. The bathroom window was too high for her to open, and was covered with a screen that she'd never get off anyway. She had a feeling she was going to be stuck in this closet until Fox carried out whatever he had planned. He had told the bus driver he was going to kill her in front of William, but she hoped William wouldn't let him do that. She grabbed and ate the pizza quickly before he might change his mind and take it back. "I'm still hungry," she yelled when she was done eating the pizza slice.

"That's it!" came an unsympathetic, blunt reply.

Heidi thought for a few minutes. He had made her lie on the floor of the car, so she had no idea where she was when they arrived in the dark, but she did remember bumping into a food dispenser as he shoved her before him on their way to the room. The food dispenser in the building was directly outside their door. "There's a food dispenser just outside the door. Can I have something from it?"

"What do you want?" came an impatient growl.

"I don't know. I'd have to see what it has. It's just outside the door. I can't run away."

The closet door swung open and Fox's pale blue eyes glared at her as he fished in his pocket for coins. "Not worth a damn penny, you are. Not worth a penny." He unlocked the door and stood in the doorway, watching her as she stood in front of the food dispenser, pretending to slowly make her choice.

"You've got one more second to choose," he warned.

"I'm a girl," she flipped back. "We take longer to decide than boys." She slid her fingers into her pocket and withdrew a fistful of notes. "Okay this one." She deposited her coins and bent down to pick the chocolate bar out of the dispenser bucket. As she did so, she dropped a handful of folded tissue notes into the dispenser bucket. The next person who used the machine would definitely discover the notes.

Liberty sat at the kitchen table in the Enns household. Felicity sat across from her, looking as if she had not combed her hair in a week. Her mother and father sat glum and guilt ridden on each side of Felicity, their arms about her shoulders in comfort. Gary Feddin pulled out a chair beside the other three, and sat a distance from Liberty, as if he was too angry to associate closely with his fiancé.

"I warned you, didn't I?" the doctor lashed out at Liberty. He had been waiting days to unload his frustration. Never in his life had he risen his voice to Liberty, but now he was in a foul state of mind.

"Whoa!" Mike interrupted, and put a hand on Gary's shoulder to quiet him. "We all knew William was messed up in something bad. We're all guilty of trying to help him. We should have protected Heidi more. I blame myself for that more than anyone."

Tears dropped down Liberty's face and washed over the

diamond ring on her hand. Gary reached out and grabbed her hand and pulled the ring from her finger, slamming it down in the middle of the table. "Was it worth it? Was a little bravo excitement worth Heidi's life? Was it?"

Felicity stood up, leaned over and picked up the ring. "Hush, Gary. You're upset, like the rest of us. You know how much Liberty loves that child. Now you take this ring and you put it back on the best thing that ever happened in your life." She opened Gary's clenched fist and pressed the ring into the palm of his hand.

Gary leaned back in his chair and put both hands on the top of his head in frustration. He couldn't remember ever getting so upset in his life. "Do you know who they'll bring her body to? They'll bring her to the doctor. They'll bring her to me." The moment the words left his mouth, he turned quickly to Liberty's sister and apologized. "I'm sorry. I didn't mean to say that. That was really selfish of me."

Liberty reached out and touched his arm. "We have to stay strong. We have to believe..."

"...certainly not in your super hero who caused this whole mess." Gary cut Liberty's sentence off sharply, and withdrew his arm from her touch.

Felicity walked around the table and stood behind Gary's chair. She leaned over and wrapped her arms around Gary's neck and laid her cheek softly on the top of his head. "Hush now! Heidi wouldn't want us fighting and blaming each other. We have to pull together. We all love Heidi... even William. Love will bring her back to us...It will. It will."

The doctor sighed as if he had used up all his anger, and now he looked calmly at the ring in his palm and reached out for Liberty's hand to replace it.

"I'm sorry, Liberty. That wasn't me talking." He shook his

head at himself. "It's just that...that little girl has wound her way into my heart."

"She has a way of doing that." Liberty smiled sadly.

Gary had the ring at Liberty's fingertip when she withdrew her hand from him. Liberty looked him sadly in the eye. "My dearest friend, I can't marry you." Liberty rose from the table in great sorrow, and kissed his cheek gently. "Right now, I feel very sick and I must lie down." She left to seek the solitude of her bedroom.

"Go after her," Felicity coaxed the doctor.

Gary looked at Felicity and ran one finger gently down Felicity's tear-stained cheek. "You're a good sister...but I think we both know who her heart belongs to." He looked at the engagement ring held between his fingertips. "It never shone as brightly as him."

Felicity's eyes misted over. "That's a matter of opinion," she said with a hushed voice, and Gary looked at her strangely. Why did Felicity always know how to get to him?

As evening dragged on, Heidi became bored with her empty closet space, and was anxious for some conversation, even if it meant talking to the enemy. She yelled out to Fox, "It's rude to read other people's diaries, you know." Fox didn't answer, so she continued, "Didn't your mother teach you any manners?"

The door flung open. "My mother taught me if I kept flapping my lips, I'd get them slapped off my face. Now shut up!" He slammed the door again.

"Maybe that's why you're such a grump," Heidi yelled bravely through the closet door. "Anyhow, people's diaries are private and I just thought you should know that...You know, it's awful boring in here. You could have at least given me a comic to read, or something. You're watching TV. Can I come out and watch? Otherwise, I just might go crazy and start kicking the walls or something. They say animals that get caged up too long start acting like that and..."

The closet door flung open again and he stood above her like a mighty statue, cold and hard as concrete. He pointed to an armchair without saying a word, and she got up off the floor and plunked herself in the armchair, facing the television set.

After watching hockey for an hour, Heidi mumbled, "Is there anything on besides hockey?"

Fox threw her a silent look of warning. Heidi shrugged her shoulders, "Hockey is fine too."

After a time, Heidi's eyes became heavy. She wondered if anyone had found her notes that she had put in the food dispenser, and why William wasn't busting in the door to rescue her by now. She finally fell asleep in the armchair. Fox left her there. He picked up a blanket to cover her with and then, bitterness boiled in him again and he flung the blanket away and let her sleep cold and uncovered.

In the morning, he was awake long before her. She stretched from her awkward position on the armchair, and watched him write a note on a piece of paper. He left the paper in plain view on the dresser. Then he turned to her, "Grab your coat! Let's go!"

"I have to go to the bathroom first."

"Make it snappy!"

"Where are we going?"

He looked at her with evil eyes, "Flying lessons." Then from his pocket, he withdrew a couple of her tissue notes and scattered them like snowflakes at her feet.

Heidi's face fell in complete defeat.

"I've got to give you credit though," Fox said. "It was a good idea. Might have worked too if I hadn't felt like an orange juice this morning. Actually, I used a few of your little notes this morning before you woke up. I slipped them underneath every door occupied in this dump. Your hero should be on his way here any minute, if one of them took heed to your notes. Hit the bathroom and then we're out of here." He pulled on a long, tan-colored, winter coat. "You've got ten seconds, and then I'll drag you out of there, pants up or down."

Heidi hurried into the bathroom. She didn't have time to write any more notes. She didn't have time to think of a plan. She exited, put on her coat and he shoved her out the door and into his car before she could pull up the zipper on the coat.

As their car flew down the highway, Heidi turned to him, "Who won the hockey game last night? It was tied when I fell asleep." She thought if she could get him to like her even a little, maybe he wouldn't harm her.

"Don't know and don't care," he snapped.

"I used to play hockey on a girls' team. Did you know that? I played defense, so I never scored much, but I stopped a lot of goals, so that's just as important, huh?"

Dr. Dwight Fox didn't reply, so Heidi kept up her chatter. "I also play the piano. Did you know that? And Grampa is teaching me to ride a horse. Can you ride a horse?"

Fox turned his head and glared at her. "Do you ever shut up?"   "I guess I could try if it would make you happy."

"Nothing makes me happy."

Heidi meditated for a few minutes. "If you're not happy, then you should get a cat." She folded her hands obediently on her lap and didn't say another word.

Fox turned into an airport and dragged her out of the car. His eyes scanned the fleet of planes, as if looking for a certain one. From the trunk of his car, he opened a long suitcase and withdrew a powerful rifle. He tucked it underneath his long coat, so that it was not visible, and told Heidi to walk in front of him, and not utter one word. In his other hand, he held a smaller gun, which he lowered into his pocket with his fingers around the trigger for immediate use.

Heidi sensed that now was not the time to disobey him. She walked before him, as he had instructed, and they approached a guarded and locked side gate. Fox stood at the gate entrance and called to the security guard who stood a few feet away. "The child is wondering what kind of plane that is." Fox nodded towards a small cargo plane landing on the far strip.

The guard smiled and walked closer to speak to Heidi. Fox withdrew his pistol and ordered him to unlock the gate.

The security guard shook his head. "I don't have keys. It's all done electronically from control."

"Then tell them to open it, and if you make a slip, the child loses her head. Understand?"

The guard retrieved a cell phone from his belt. Fox instructed Heidi to dial the numbers, then handed the phone back to the guard.
"They'll know something is wrong," he said. "I have no legal reason for opening the gate."

"Think fast." Fox snarled, and the guard swallowed as he spoke to control," Can you unlock B3? Yes ...well, I...have a diplomat...who is supposed to be on Flight...." He glanced at Fox for further input.

With the pistol in his hand, Fox quickly gestured towards a smaller plane on the runway.

"Flight 452. Yes, I know he's supposed to... Yes, I know." He sighed and with frightened eyes, the guard informed Fox, "They say you still have to go through security inside before you can get on the plane."

Fox pointed the gun at his head. "Then tell them there's a gun between your eyeballs, and if they don't open this gate, you and this child are history. Oh, and I want one pilot on the plane. No one else, and one parachute handy at the exit door of the plane. Don't get cute tampering with the parachute as the child will be using it. After I get airborne, you can have your pilot and plane back...all safe and sound, if they do everything I say." He opened up his coat to reveal the high powered rifle. "And just in case someone wants to get heroic, I can point this gun at any one of those planes loaded with people for takeoff, and blow them clean off the tarmac."

The guard relayed the message and B3 Gate opened.

When the phone call came, Donna Enns screamed for Felicity. Felicity grabbed the phone and spoke to the stranger on the other end of the phone. "Yes, Yes!" Felicity cried. "It's true. Yes, she's been kidnapped. Oh, thank God you found her note. Did you see what direction they went, what make of car, anything?"

Once Felicity ended her conversation with the caller, Liberty took over the phone and contacted Constable Fluery, who immediately contacted Jo Wong. William had not returned from Spain with Jo Wong and Liberty, so she had no idea where

William was at this moment, but Liberty knew Wong would have that information.

Within half an hour, the new local banker showed up on Enn's doorstep. It was not until he peeled off his mask, that they realized the banker was William in disguise. "Let me handle Fox," he advised Mike Enns.

"No," Mike disagreed. "I think you have done quite enough. If this man sees you, Heidi is dead. Simple as that."

"You don't understand," William argued. "It's a game to him. If I'm not involved, there's no satisfaction for him. He won't hurt her until I am there to witness it. I have to find them before he knows I'm around." William walked to the window and looked across to the snow-covered hills. "Wong is going to call me the second they get into the hotel room. I'm sure Fox will leave clues as to where he's taken Heidi. He'll want me to follow."

Donna poured a round of coffee as they waited anxiously for Jo Wong's call from the motel. William sat silently, and kept his eyes lowered to the tablecloth. He knew the family blamed him for Heidi's abduction and found it difficult to face them. Felicity had nodded hello to him but had not spoken one word since his arrival. He hadn't seen Liberty at all, and Donna moved about with a quiet sadness that broke his heart.

"Did Liberty get back from Spain okay?" William finally asked, worried that he had not seen her this morning.

Mike nodded. "She's back...just lying down. We didn't know you were both in Spain."

William nodded in return. It had only been a couple weeks since he had been trampled by the stallion, and he had suffered barely any sleep or rest between flights to Spain and Germany and back to Canada again. He was exhausted and every inch of his body ached. The throbbing from the concussion was worsened by too much air travel and stress, and his broken bones had barely had time to heal. He leaned his elbow on the table and cupped his forehead in one hand. For a second, sleep overwhelmed him and his hand slipped from his forehead, causing him to nearly hit his head on the table.

"Hey, son. You better lie down," Mike ordered, "or you'll give yourself another concussion."

William shook his head in refusal, and took another sip of coffee.

Mike tried to make conversation to keep William awake. "Bill Hogkins dropped by here yesterday. We didn't tell him about Heidi being kidnapped. Thought it best to keep quiet or the media would be all over this...maybe frighten Fox into doing something drastic. Oh, and Bill said he's been trying to get the banker to extend his credit for three years with no luck, and then this new banker shows up for a day while Jerry's on vacation and gives him the money without asking for any collateral at all. Bill was on cloud nine, hitting for a cattle sale yesterday."

William gave a slight smile. "Let's hope the cattle market holds for a few years."

Mike grinned back at William's generous deed.

Liberty twisted her fingers under the water tap in the bathroom. It felt strange not to have Gary's ring on her finger. She was not aware that William had arrived and so a relieved smile crossed her face at finding him sat at the kitchen table.

Minutes later, William's cell phone rang and the anxious voice of Wong conveyed Fox's message. "He's left you a note. It says, "*Meet me at Grandvalley Basin at thirteen hours sharp. Bring the family!*"

William inhaled deeply. "What do you think he has planned?" he asked Jo Wong, knowing that whatever the plan was, it would be without mercy.

"Fluery says the local police just confirmed the hijacking of a plane from the Grandvalley airport about five minutes ago. I hope you're not thinking what I am."

William snapped the cell shut and looked at Mike. "Grandvalley Basin" was all William said. He grabbed his jacket and ran out the door to his own car. Liberty was a step behind William and leapt into the seat beside him. Snow flew as their tires spun out of the yard. Mike and the others followed out the door equally as fast, while Felicity called Gary at the hospital to meet them part way.

The cell rang in William's pocket, and he tossed it to Liberty to answer. "It's the control tower at Grandvalley Airport. They say the hijacker of the plane wants to speak to you," Liberty stuttered, her voice shaking with fear at what Fox might have in mind.

"Put him on speaker," William said, knowing the words would not be what he wanted to hear.

"William Casson, I'm going to teach the kid to fly."

"Don't do it, Dwight," William begged. "It's me you want, not some innocent little girl."

"Well now! Didn't I heard those same words come out of my very own mouth when you were blowing my children into the sea?" Fox scoffed in irony.

"The Agency didn't know your children were in the house. I swear." William begged. "I worked beside you for months. Do you think I would honestly do that to innocent children? You know me better than that. You don't want to do this to a child."

"Look to the heavens and pray," Fox laughed, and hung up the phone.

William's face went white. He looked sadly at Liberty and shook his head. Liberty knew by the look on his face that this time William was not a miracle worker. They could do nothing but pray to One who was.

William swung into Grandvalley and stopped the car at the bottom of the valley basin where the land spread out like an oval bowl cupped inside a circle of blue hills. The Enns car pulled up beside him and everyone dismounted. No one said a word for each knew in their heart that they might be about to witness the horror of their lifetime.

William removed the sling which cupped his broken arm, and opened the trunk of the car. He withdrew a powerful rifle with a scope and laid the rifle across the top of the car for stability. Then he leaned across in readiness, one eye on the scope. No one said a word. They all knew that should Fox throw Heidi from the plane, William would shoot her before she suffered the deadly drop to earth.

They could hear the plane in the distance and knew it was approaching. Gary enveloped his arms around trembling Felicity and she buried her head against his chest, awaiting the oncoming doom. Heidi's grandparents clutched each other's hands, tears flowing silently down both of their faces. Liberty looked at William's guilt-ridden face as he put his eye close to the scope on the rifle. She thought only a very strong man would do what William was preparing to do for Heidi's sake. He mouthed silent words to her, "I'm so sorry."

Liberty silently mouthed back, "I know." Then as the plane approached, she whispered to him in a feeble little voice. "God be with your aim, chameleon...for Heidi's sake." Then she faced the sky and waited for the plane to pass overhead, both hands clutched in deepest prayer.

Heidi hadn't said a word the whole time they got on the plane and during takeoff. She remained silent as they flew for twenty minutes. She just stared out the window until she finally commented, "I think we're flying in circles because we passed that lake down there five minutes ago."

Fox looked at his watch. Then he instructed the pilot, "In eight minutes, I want you to fly over Grandvalley Basin. "He nudged him with the gun barrel. "Understand?" The pilot nodded.

Fox took off his long coat and put on the pilot's shorter jacket. He walked back to the exit door and began putting on a parachute harness.
Heidi frowned. "You told the guard back there that the parachute was for me. Whew! I'm glad you changed your mind because I really don't like heights. Oh...And when you get to where you're going, remember to get yourself a cat. If you're lonely or sad...or forgive me, Mister, for saying so...grouchy like you are, get yourself a cat."

Fox froze and stopped buckling up the harness. He lifted his eyes to stare at her innocent child face. Slowly, he slipped off the harness, reached out and grabbed her, and started putting the harness on Heidi instead.

"I can't do it," she begged in refusal. "I can't jump." He looked at his watch, opened the door of the plane and jumped out with her. As they dropped, Heidi clung to him, screaming loudly. He pulled the parachute cord and they rose and soon floated softly in the air. Heidi stopped screaming and looked into his face, afraid to look down.

"When you land, roll like a ball, so you don't break your

legs," Fox instructed her. He had originally planned to wear the parachute himself, jump from the plane with her and then let her drop to her death in front of William. But somewhere along the line, the satisfaction of killing the child hollowed, and now all he wanted was to be free of the ache in his chest for his own children. Killing this one would not free him of that.

"Where are we going?" Heidi asked, still clinging to him tightly.

"We're both going home," he smiled, and loosened her grip on his coat, and set her free. Heidi drifted away in the parachute, screaming at the top of her lungs as Fox dropped quickly from her view.

They watched the form drop from the plane, and William aimed the rifle, thinking Fox had tossed Heidi from the plane. Then the parachute opened and William hesitated as he saw both clinging to the falling parachute. No one breathed a word. Suddenly, they saw a body drop away from the parachute, and a horrible gasp escaped everyone's lips. Felicity screamed and Gary turned her eyes away, pressing her face into his shoulder. As the body fell rapidly towards earth, William aimed his scope to end Heidi's torture. Through the scope, he quickly recognized that it was Fox falling to his death. Heidi was in the parachute, not Fox.

"It's Heidi!" William rejoiced. "It's Heidi in the parachute. Come on. With the wind, it looks like she'll land to the south." He quickly unloaded the bullets from the rifle and threw the gun on the back seat of his car. All jumped in their cars and hit south, following the parachute in the sky above them.

Heidi was buried in the snow beneath a blanket of fluttering parachute when they found her. Few occasions in history could be more joyous to her family than seeing Heidi's head pop up like a gopher.

Gary insisted they immediately take her to the hospital for observation, and any chance of hypothermia or frost bite from the cold parachute ride. He wrapped her inside his jacket and carried her to the awaiting car without delay.

William remained back a distance from them, watching quietly. He had so many mixed feelings spinning inside of him; relief that Heidi was safe, happiness for her family, closure from Dwight Fox's threat, and sadness that farewells were forthcoming.

Liberty approached him slowly. "That was too close," she sighed, still wiping tears of relief from her eyes.

William smiled quietly, and put his rifle back in the trunk of the car, relieved that he had not needed to pull the trigger. "I've called Wong," he informed her. "They're picking up Fox's body...I'll take his ashes back to Spain...bury him beside his children. Figure POLLU owes him that much."

"That's kind of you...more than he'd do for you...oh, and the loan was more than Hopkins would have done for you too."

William laughed at his secret deed as banker for a day. "I know...but...something has to define me as one of the good guys to you once in awhile."

Liberty reached out and brushed a lock of hair from his forehead. "You're more than one of the good guys. I realize that now."

He noted the ring gone from her finger. "You should have kept the ring," he said sadly. "I can't stay, Lib. My destiny lies with POLLU...For the next six months, Strauz has talked me into being Assistant Captain while he has surgery. It will give me time to heal a bit, but mostly, it will give me an opportunity to alter a few policies that I have always been negative about. When he returns, I'm off to Venezuela...supposed to be a soccer player for a team owner who's illegally cutting down rain forest."

"You play soccer?"

"Aye! Pretty darn good too. But this time, I have to be the team fitness instructor, seeing as Strauz won't allow me to bounce any soccer balls off my head for a while."

They stood silent for a few moments. He looked across at the blue hills on the other side of the basin. "I think you know I can't stay. You've lost a good man in Gary."

"Yes, well, I think Felicity and Heidi have found him, so all is not a loss." She looked towards the car where Gary was wrapping Heidi in a warm car blanket with the full concern of a father. Heidi had her arms around both her mother and Gary, laughing as her grandparents promised her a million pink ponies.

Donna called out to Liberty, "Are you coming to the hospital with us or with William?"

Gary turned and looked across the distance to William. For a few silent moments, Gary searched for forgiveness towards the man that had changed their lives forever. Whoever William was, Gary decided he was on some side of justice and a man capable of martyrdom that set him apart from most. Gary rose one hand in a wave and William acknowledged with a wave back. They had no need to speak, for Gary's wave offered peace, and William accepted. It was good enough for now.

"Go with them," William insisted sadly. "Tell Heidi and your folks I said goodbye. I'm sorry. I've left you with nothing." He opened the car door reluctantly.

"Will you be home for Christmas?" she asked, her voice trembling to think she might never see him again.

"Home?" William asked, repeating the same conversation they had spoken months before when they parted.

"Yes, home," she repeated softly, her misty eyes begging him not to disappear from their lives completely.

He slipped his one hand around the back of her head. Her auburn hair dropped like waterfalls through his fingers and he thought of how dearly he would love to run his fingers through her soft inviting curls every night. He was about to kiss her on the lips but that would have hinted at the possibility of his return, and he could promise nothing. So he kissed her on the cheek as softly as a feather, slid into his car and drove away without saying another word.

Six months passed and late one June day, a familiar voice spoke behind Heidi's back as she practiced her piano lessons in the Enns farm house. "That should have been an F Sharp."

Heidi spun on the piano bench to see William standing there with Cleo hugging close to his pant leg. She swung her knees up on the bench and leaped into William's arms. "You've come back!"

"Only until tomorrow." Seeing Heidi's face fall in disappointment, he added, "But I promise to be back for Christmas."

"But I'll be all grown up by then, and Kitkat won't be a kitten anymore." She pointed to the half-grown orange kitten that William had rescued from the loft fall.

William sighed. "Okay, I'll visit you...in September when the golden rods are blooming... but keep that a secret...and make sure you hit F Sharp the next time I hear you play that piece. Where's Liberty?"

"She just ran to the barn to check on a mare that's having a foal."

William's eyes turned to look out the living room

window towards the barn. "Did she ever get back together with Gary?"

"No...Mom and Gary are dating now. He's kind of neat when you get to know him. Doctors save people's lives every day, you know."

William smiled to see her growing affection for a man who would soon become her father. He turned to look out the window at the barn again.

Heidi caught his arm. "How did you know I hit the wrong note? Can you play the piano?" She could hardly restrain her excitement at the thought.

William turned his head to look in all directions, making sure no other persons were about. "Can you keep a secret?" he whispered. Heidi bobbed her head up and down in anticipation.

He sat down on the piano bench and Heidi snuggled close beside him. William raised both hands above the keys. For a moment his fingers hovering over the keys as if apprehensive to reveal his secret. Then he began playing Beethoven's sonata, *Fur Elise* with the skill of a fine pianist. The music floated through the air and reached Liberty's ears as she returned from the barn.

She knew instantly that it could not be Heidi playing the piano, as the nine year old was not at such an advanced level in her music. Liberty quietly opened the door to the kitchen and tip-toed to the archway between the kitchen and living room to see who was playing the music. Her eyes beheld William seated beside Heidi at the piano. Cleo's two front feet were up on the piano bench, also watching William's fingers fly like magic over the piano keys. Liberty smiled at the threesome, and listened in awe at William's breath-taking talent.

A bouquet of red roses from their garden sat on a table near Liberty, and as he finished the sonata, she withdrew one single rose and walked slowly forward. Suddenly, he became awareness of her presence and turned to watch her approach.

"You once said there were roses in everyone if we ever came close enough to see them," Liberty said softly. She rested the rose stem gently on top of the piano in recognition of the many roses that lie hidden inside him. "I have a feeling this is one of those times."

They stared at each other for a long moment. It was the first time that William remembered feeling like a fragile glass house. "The Agency doesn't know I can play the piano," he revealed quietly. "I learned from watching Tony play, but not even he knew. Playing the piano was sort of something that...I made of myself...not something they made me into. I kept it a secret, so whenever I felt lost in the million of characters I was trained to be...that I could find myself." He gave a short laugh. "I guess that sounds ridiculous."

"No, not at all," she spoke almost in a whisper. "I'm just glad I got to see the real William before POLLU whisks you away again." A tear glistened in her eye.

William answered with an uneasy voice. "I was wondering...if you might like Venezuela at this time of year?"

Liberty was shocked for a moment, then reasoning crossed her mind. "What comes after Venezuela? You're a poet one day and a pirate, the next. Where would that leave me?"

"Well, you can think about it...until tomorrow morning. Come spend some time with me...like a vacation...Get to know me better. Think of it as an adventure. Then maybe, if you can put up with a chameleon, you might consent to be my wife."

Her eyes widened in surprise at the marriage proposal. "I...I don't know if I can live like that. I need roots, William. I want my children to have roots."

"And roots you shall have. Strauz likes this arrangement

of Wong and I based in Glenfield...likely because I would be stationed on the other side of the ocean from him and his policies." He laughed slightly and rose from the piano bench. "This would be our home, even if I'm gone a lot, but you would always have family around you here, and you could always confide in Wong's wife."

Heidi had sat still and quiet long enough. Now she blurted in. "Say yes, Aunt Liberty. If you don't marry him, I will."

Both William and Liberty laughed. William wrapped one arm around Heidi and gave her a little hug. "See, I have a second offer, Liberty, so you better not wait too long or I'll be taken by another beautiful lady."

"But I'm afraid I will spend too many nights wondering where you are and if you are safe."

William understood her fears and knew he could never completely erase them. "I have a feeling you will do that anyway, whether you are married to me or not."

Liberty acknowledged agreement with the nod of her head.

William then dug deep in his coat pocket and withdrew a breathtaking ring. A band of white diamonds circled a magnificent aurora borealis solitaire. The multi-colors rayed off the stone like the Northern Lights.

Liberty's mouth opened in awe. "Oooh! It's beautiful...like...like a chameleon." She suddenly realized the significance of the ring's chosen stones.

William slipped the ring on her finger. "This way when I am gone from your sight, you need only look down at your hand and you will see me with you always." This time, there was no kissing Liberty on the cheek. This time, his lips touched hers and promised her everything.

www.ingramcontent.com/pod-product-compliance
Lightning Source LLC
Chambersburg PA
CBHW050324200626
46810CB00023B/3051